Panda Books
The Story of Qiuju

Chen Yuanbin was born in Anhui in 1955. Following middle school he worked successively as farmer, postman, accountant, typist and legal worker. Since 1980, when he began his literary career, he has written prolifically and many of his works have won prizes. He belongs to the Anhui Provincial Literary and Art Association, and is a member of the Chinese Writers' Association, and the Anhui Legal Society.

Chen Yuanbin

The Story of Qiuju

Panda Books

Panda Books
First Edition 1995
Second Printing 1997

Copyright © 1991 by CHINESE LITERATURE PRESS
ISBN 7−5071−0277−7
ISBN 0−8351−3144−0

Published by CHINESE LITERATURE PRESS
Beijing 100037, China
Distributed by China International Book Trading Corporation
35 Chegongzhuang Xilu, Beijing 100044, China
P.O. Box 399, Beijing, China
Printed in the People's Republic of China

CONTENTS

Preface

Chen Yuanbin

IT is through my writing that I express my thoughts about the world…

In 1955 on the 29th day of the twelveth month according to the lunar calendar I was born in a small town in Anhui Province. My father once served as the town head. Of him I clearly recall that one day, he took me to fish with him in a pond, a pond overgrown with green moss on its banks. From the early morning we lowered our net into the water and pulled it up again and again each time finding that the only thing caught in it was water reed. I thought of our efforts as labour lost, but my father was persistant. He kept lowering and pulling the net until sunset when we finally caught a big fish. His tenacity astounded me. My mother, director of a small factory, was a soberminded and very decisive woman. She was the person who made the final decision at each important step the family took. The characters of my parents moulded me and subsequently found their way into my works. When "Celestial River" was published, Lei Da, a literary critic based in Beijing described it as being: "Written with a sober mind and a steady, easy manner. 'Celestial River' is a work impressive for the depth of meaning it contains. The author seems to tell us objectively of what he observes from a distance. As in his tales he tells the facts, not his personal feeling, his narration is doubly effective, his stories more poignant." Lei Da's words express what it is I seek to achieve in my writing. However, I feel that perhaps he praised "Celestial River" too highly as a fictional story with the background of contemporary life. "Heaven's Course", another story published later, was more deserving of this compliment. As this story unfolds several legal cases criss-cross over each other drawing the reader in. At the present time in China, most stories based on, or containing, legal cases fall into the category of mere sensationalism or sensual stimulation. My aim was to lift stories based on legal cases to the higher echelons of literature. I began this process in 1988, after I graduated from Lu Xun Literary Academy in Beijing. Since then, I have written a dozen or more stories of this kind to be published in different magazines and have been repeatedly awarded for my efforts. These stories constitute that part of my work with which I am most satisfied, and which I consider to be most representative of my writing. On the whole literature woven around legal themes has been little utilised and explored in present-day China and successful writers in this field are few. Upon the publication of "Heaven's Course", Zhou Jieren based in Shanghai commented: "The credit for the success of this story goes to its unique subject matter and approach." This story however, is not as important to me as "The Story of Qiuju", my most successful piece of writing which also has won me the greatest fame.

After being adapted for film by the talented director Zhang Yimou, and starring the well-known actress

Gong Li, "The Story of Qiuju" won the Golden
Lion Prize at the 49th Venice International Film Festival. My urge to write this story was also quite unlike
that which inspired other work: On a cold winter morning, just before I started for a reservoir construction
site, I heard the news that the apartment building in
the provincial city, the building in which I lived, had
caught on fire. I rushed back from the distant countryside but all I saw upon my return were piles of debris
and smoke. All my belongings were gone. I felt
unusually calm and was suddenly struck by the urge
to write a story. I finished the story in a little room in
a noisy hotel where I stayed temporarily. I planned to
write a novelette based on a short story that could be
told in one sentence, an appealing story from a country woman's limited perspective, related in colloquial
language, a natural and unrestrained narrative which
payed close attention to both the feeling and the quali-
ty of the language. I decided on an unconventional approach: leaving out anything that was not directly asso-
ciated to the case. With so much to concentrate on I
had not made my work easy for myself on this task,
because I believed a unique work was born in pain but
created many difficulties. The story was first published
in *Chinese Writers,* occupying a prominent position . It
received a warm reception and topped the list of literary
winners. Following the success of the film, China's
Ministry of Post and Telecommunications issued a
commemorative envelope to mark its international ac-
claim, with photos of Gong Li, Zhang Yimou and myself, an unprecedented practice in Chinese stamp col-
lecting history. "The Story of Qiuju" expressed my
own state of mind with regard to personal experiences,

and my own response to being injured.

So far, I have published many works, sixteen of which have been translated and published in different languages. Although representing only a small part of my work, hopefully the four stories contained in this book will enable me to communicate more fully with audiences in English speaking and other nations.

The Story of Qiuju

THE sun had warmed up. Qiuju was shovelling the last spadeful of pond sludge over the wheat field when she heard the news that her husband had been beaten up. She packed up, went home to see how he was, and then went straight to the village head.

He lived at the eastern end of the village in a house with two wings and a courtyard, a blue, brick building with a slate threshold and a roof of small tiles. In the courtyard there was a well shaded by a trellis of shrivelled vines. Opposite this were pots of flowers reduced to mere dry stalks. A dog was tied up. Qiuju steered clear of it and looked into the central room. The village head was inside, drinking.

She demanded, "You hit him! I've got the proof, and the doctor's report. What have you got to say for yourself?"

The village head snorted, "Huh!"

"You may well hit him, kick him in the stomach, but you kicked him in his privates! It could have been fatal! Don't you have anything to say?"

The village head raised his glass slowly.

"Well, don't say I didn't warn you," said Qiuju.

"What can you do to me?" sneered the village head.

"Let the government settle the matter," she answered.

"It wasn't a private fight. I'm the village head. If

the government doesn't side with me, who is going to look after things around here?''

"Just you wait!" said Qiuju angrily.

"Suit yourself. You know the way into town? Take the ferry across the reservoir, walk ten or twenty *li* and there you are. It's not an easy trip.''

Seeing that he was becoming abusive, she said no more and left. After walking a *li* or two she reached the ferry. Everyone else was already aboard and the boatman was untying the vessel ready to move off. At Qiuju's shout, he held onto the rope until she had boarded. "Stand firm," he said, picking up a punting pole to push the boat slowly out to the middle of the reservoir.

The passengers were all talking, some sitting down, others standing around with their hands thrust into their pockets, their luggage stored in the cabin. The boatman smiled. "Once the new road's finished, you won't bother with my boat any more, will you? Mind you, it's not going to be much more than a mud track and most of it will be outside the province, well out of your way. It won't be as good as the boat!''

One passenger said, "Wangqiao Village has been part of Anhui for generations. The reservoir obstructs roads, so that we're now part of Jiangsu Province. Getting out of here is harder than climbing up to heaven. It would be better if we belonged to Jiangsu.''

The boatman's eyes fell on Qiuju. "Haven't I seen you before?'' he asked.

"She's from the Wan family, wife of Wan Shanqing,'' said one.

"I see, no wonder you look worried,'' he said to her. "Are you going to bring a law suit against the village head? A saying goes 'Avoid the court when possible'. How on earth have things got as far as this?"

Qiuju replied: "A village is like a big family. The head can give orders, beat and shout at his subordinates; but isn't it going too far when you nearly kill someone? What's more, when I went to talk to him he wouldn't even explain."

"He's in the wrong," the boatman nodded.

At this point, the boat began to wobble. As they approached the middle of the reservoir, they felt water spraying their faces. The calm disappeared and a wind rushed across the surface of the water biting icily at the passengers' faces and churning up rolling waves as it grew stronger and colder.

"Where there's water, there's wind; and where there's wind, there are waves," said the boatman. "It'll calm down in a moment." He put down the pole and began to row his oars. The wind howled and the deck rocked underfoot. Suddenly everyone fell silent except for an occasional whisper. People held their breath, slowly exhaling to calm their heart-beats. The boatman rowed faster. They were soon past the windy patch and heading for the shore. The boat gradually steadied and the boatman switched his oars for the punting pole again. When the boat reached the shore, they disembarked and went their different ways.

The town was not its former self. There was a new gravel road with trees and buildings on either side —— an eye-straining distance from one end to the other. The buildings were different sizes and heights. Qiuju assumed that a six-storeyed building was the local government offices, but on entering discovered it was a factory. After several twists and turns, she eventually found it in an out-of-the-way corner. The local government occupied two rows of one-storeyed buildings. Qiuju entered a door where someone took her to the westernmost room and introduced her.

"Li's in charge of public security. Tell him your story." Li was a plain-looking man in his early forties. From his face, she could not decide if he was honest or crafty. He was holding a narrow-waisted teacup in both hands and reading a newspaper. He turned around to look at her.

"Wang Changzhu?" he said. "Did he send you to invite me over for a drink? Tell him to correct his bad manners at table or I won't go!"

"I've come to report him."

"Oh?" Li was startled. He examined the medical report and the written evidence she had set before him and frowned.

"What's this? This is from a district hospital in Jiangsu Province."

"The roads from Wangqiao to Anhui Province are blocked. I had to go to Jiangsu," Qiuju explained.

On hearing the whole story, Li tidied up the documents and looked at his watch.

"The canteen's open now," he said. "You can eat here."

She politely declined, but he insisted, saying, "It's not on me. I'll help you buy the coupons. They've got chopsticks and bowls that you can use."

"It's all right, thanks. I saw lots of restaurants on my way here."

"They cheat you at places like that," Li said.

"I've already asked: a bowl of noodles is fifty or

sixty fen. Not that expensive.''

Li stood up and said, "I've got a meeting this afternoon. I'll deal with this matter tomorrow. Go home and wait.''

Just before lunchtime the next day Li came to find her.

"Sorry to have given you this trouble. Did you walk here?'' Qiuju said to him.

"No, I cycled.''

"On the new road?''

"No, that's too far. I'm quite a good cyclist, so I came through the fields and then caught the boat. I got half way to your village before deciding that pushing the bike uphill was too much effort, so I took it all the way back and left it with the boatman and then walked here. So it took me a long time to get here.''

Qiuju was surprised. "You mean you haven't seen the village head yet?''

"I'll see your husband first.''

After Li had seen the injuries, they headed for the village head's house. The dog barked savagely as they approached and the village head yelled at it to be quiet. "Have a seat,'' he called to Li. Then, on seeing Qiuju, his face fell and he went quiet. Li went in, sat down and bade Qiuju and the village head to sit down too. Both declined. Li then said, "I've seen the doctor's report, the witness' statements and the man's injuries. The fact is you are in the wrong.''

The village head lost his temper. "What do you mean I'm in the wrong! Did I do it for personal gain? This village has been ordered to grow rape. Everyone agreed — everyone except this one man. All the fields around his are full of rape. His is the only one with wheat in it. It's like a scab on the head. When the investigation group saw it, they took points away from the village as a whole. And they ordered us to change the crop within a specified time. I advised him a thousand times to change his mind, but he wouldn't listen to reason! What else could I do but kick him?''

Li laughed. "Well, you should have used your tongue more.''

"Maybe I should have used my teeth!''

"Whatever you say, you did hit and injure him," Li remarked gravely.

The village head glared at him resentfully. "Are you speaking on your own behalf or on behalf of the township?''

Li turned to Qiuju. "Would you leave us alone for a while?''

She waited outside until Li came out with a proposal. ''The village will pay your husband's medical costs. Apart from that, he'll get convalescence expenses and a sickness subsidy. The village will pay half and the village head will pay the other half. What do you think?''

Qiuju said, "But what will people think? That I'm just after the money! I want nothing but a public apology.''

"He's rather arrogant," said Li, "and he's the village head. He won't want to lose face.''

"So what?''

Li thought for a while and then suggested, "The fact that he's going to fork out the money proves he's in the wrong. Can't you take that as an apology?'' Qiuju thought this over and eventually agreed.

Back inside, Li said, "Right, we'll deal with it in this way then. Let's call it 'making peace' rather than 'a reprimand'. If we're all agreed and everything is back to normal, I'll stay here and eat with you. If not, I'll go home starving!"

He did have dinner in the village. Afterwards he said a few more words to Qiuju and made his way back into town.

"Who's just been here?" Qiuju's husband called out from his sick bed.

"Someone named Li from public security," she answered, and then added, "I reported the village head and won."

"Are you quite sure?" asked her husband anxiously.

"Li said I was right and he was wrong." Then she told him about the money. "He's going to pay us this afternoon. We're to take that as an apology."

That afternoon, Qiuju went to look for the village head once more. The dog was barking again. When the village head told it to be quiet, there seemed to be an underlying edge in his tone of voice.

"I've brought the receipts," said Qiuju.

"How much is it altogether?" He looked at the figures and then took out a wad of new notes. He counted them one by one and then counted again. Qiuju was waiting to receive the money and say, "Fine, let's leave it at that." But before she had time to say anything, the village head flung the money on the floor.

Qiuju was quite bewildered. "What are you doing?"

"Giving you money," he sneered.

"You beat my husband and refused to apologize, and now you insult me!"

"I'm being perfectly reasonable." He paused for a minute and then said, "I'm still the village head. I'm still in charge of the ups and downs of this village. I could cause your family an awful lot of trouble if I so wished. There are thirty notes on the floor, you can bow your head each time you pick one up. That means you are making thirty apologies. Then I'll forget the whole business." Having said that, he urged her to bend down and pick up the money. Qiuju said angrily, "What about what you said this morning?"

"What did I say?"

"You made no objection."

The village head laughed. "Do you think I'm that soft? Li had cycled through fields to get here this morning. It wasn't an easy journey. I wanted to show him respect. Anyway, all this money has come out of village funds. None of it came out of my own pocket."

Qiuju stared dumbly at him and then walked over the money and out of his house.

At home she sat down and told her husband what had happened.

"I thought you couldn't really beat him," he said.

"Why didn't you say so before?"

"I don't know."

"Well, you should have," Qiuju snorted angrily.

"This is all very awkward," sighed her husband.

For quite a while she was speechless and distracted. "If we don't get this cleared up, life won't be worth living."

"But what if we lose?"

Qiuju spoke through clenched teeth, "I'll take

enough money and go into town and stay there until it's sorted out." The couple tossed and turned in bed for a whole night without sleeping a wink.

She got up at first light, washed, made her way over the icy ground, took the ferry and went to town. Li's office was locked. On asking where he was, she was told that he had gone to a meeting in the county town and would probably be away for a couple of days. Qiuju wondered what to do. She thought about their first meeting two days before and suddenly remembered that the public security person and the village head were friends. Had the pair of them set a trap for her? She thought about it and decided the only way out was to go to the county police.

She caught the daily bus to town. When she got off, the bus station was full of people. The winter sun was unusually warm and the morning ice had already melted. There were several shabby old rooms in the bus station, all unfamiliar to her. None of the passengers queued in the bus shelter. Instead, they crowded in front of it in the wind. The surrounding fence had two gates: a small gate for passengers and a larger one for buses. Qiuju stood still trying to relax and looked around to get her bearings. Then she pushed her way out and followed the road into town.

Everything looked quite different from seven or eight years before. There were now so many food stalls that the streets had narrowed. All the stall-holders shouted their wares: wonton soup, dumplings, noodles, sheep innards, smoked rabbit heads, stewed pig tails in soy sauce... Qiuju asked a kindly stall-holder for directions. "Are you eating?" he inquired in a thin voice. When he realized that she was only asking for directions, his smile disappeared and he merely gestured towards a building. Qiuju followed some rather proud-looking people into the building but was stopped at the gate by an old man.

"You have to register to come in here. Have you got your ID card?"

He checked her identity card and asked her business. She was interrupted before she could finish her sentence. "This is the court-house. The police station is further down the road."

"Which way?"

"Go straight ahead, turn right, then left, then right again. You'll see a big gate. Inside the gate is an office building. Go to the first floor, third room on the left and give your written complaint to someone in there."

Qiuju did not understand. "What written complaint?"

"A piece of paper saying whom you're making an accusation against and why," the old man explained.

Qiuju looked panic-stricken. "Oh, no! I didn't bring that!"

"Don't worry," the old man reassured her. "You can get one written for you."

The street was packed with traders selling everything imaginable: pots, bowls, gourds, plates, spoons, oil, salt, sauces, tea, things to eat, things to use, things to wear... Qiuju turned a corner and the next street was full of wool sellers. They seemed to have wool of every shade of every colour: reds, greens, blues, yellows... The colours filled her eyes but her mind was preoccupied.

She crossed the street, turned a corner, and nearly walked into a writing stall. The stall was in a sunny corner well protected from the wind and its owner was a bespectacled old fellow with a goatee beard. He was bargaining with a middle-aged man. "If this was a letter to a relative or a friend, a thank-you letter, a letter asking for relief, an application for a transfer of work, then that price might just be possible, but for a letter of apology — there is no bargaining."

"But that's not a fair price," protested the middle-aged man.

"How can you complain about the price? You knocked someone over on your bike and you were caught trying to run off. It wasn't an easy letter to write, you know."

The middle-aged man sloped off, clutching his letter. Qiuju watched this scene and then went over to inquire about a written complaint.

"Certainly," said the stall-holder. He unrolled a sheet of paper and took up a pen. Qiuju told him her story and by the time she had finished, the stall-holder had finished writing.

Qiuju took her letter to the police station and found the third room on the left as instructed. Inside, two uniformed men sat talking, with narrow-waisted teacups in hand. Qiuju handed over her complaint. One of the men took it and looked at it, frowned, and then passed it to the other man who also frowned and said, "The language is rather ornate, isn't it? And the claims seem somewhat exaggerated. And the major facts aren't clear at all. To be honest, it's no good whatsoever. Did you have this written at the stall outside? How much did he charge you?"

"He wanted forty. I gave him thirty-five,' replied Qiuju.

The two men exchanged glances. "We're so busy at the moment, everything's rather a mess. We ought to take some time to clear up the streets a little," said one of the men. The other said to Qiuju:

"You ought to go to the Lawyer's Office for this sort of thing."

"Why?"

"They help people bring cases to court. They'll write indictments, represent you in a lawsuit, speak in your defence, lodge an appeal for you and so on, in all types of cases — criminal, civil, economic or political."

"Is it publicly owned?" asked Qiuju.

The other man then attempted to explain the situation as simply as he could, and she listened attentively. When he had finished, she asked the two men to give her directions in detail.

The Lawyer's Office was a single-storey building with five rooms of different sizes. At the extreme east and west ends, doors opened onto a corridor. Halfway down was a large double door with three white plaques all covered in thick and thin black characters. It certainly lacked the grandeur of the Court and Public Security Bureau buildings and she stood gazing at it for a while. She consulted the woman in the westernmost room who pointed to the middle room without even looking up from her paper. Inside, several people were sitting at desks. Qiuju was directed to the man at the corner desk.

The man was less than thirty but already had a few grey hairs. He gestured her to a seat with his narrow-waisted cup.

"How should I address you?" she asked when she sat down.

"My name is Wu. Call me Little Wu, or Lawyer Wu as you prefer."

"Lawyer Wu," said Qiuju.

"Do you wish to engage an attorney?" asked Lawyer Wu.

"What does that mean?"

"Someone to represent you, be present at all occasions and defend your interests according to law."

"Would I have to pay for that?"

"Of course you would," the lawyer said, frowning, and added, "The money goes to the state, not into our pockets. The prices are fixed," and he took a form out to show her. She asked him to explain very carefully.

"After hiring the lawyer at fixed rate, you would also have to pay for the travel, food and hotel expenses for any outside investigation, documentation and certification that may be necessary."

"How much? Roughly?"

"It's hard to say. We'd have to look at the actual situation. You pay whatever is spent."

Qiuju bowed her head, silently calculating. Failing to work it out, she finally asked, "What if I didn't hire an attorney but just had an indictment written? Would that be all right?"

"Certainly."

The indictment was surprisingly cheap. Only now did she realize that the stall-holder really had cheated her. Suppressing her regret, she retold her story to Lawyer Wu who wrote the indictment accordingly. She paid and rushed over to the police station. It was already closed.

That lunchtime Qiuju ate a bowl of noodles so spicy that they made her break out in a sweat. By the time her sweat had dried, the sun was low in the sky. On her way back to the police station, she inquired about accommodation. Her first stop was a small inn on a street corner and she asked how much they charged. The man at the registration desk stuck his head through the window and asked, "With or without a receipt?"

"How much with and how much without?"

He laughed. "If you want a receipt, it will say six yuan and you can pay only four, so when you get six yuan refund from your office, you'd have made two yuan a night. If you are paying for yourself and do not need a receipt, it'll be three yuan a night."

Qiuju was astonished. "Is this place privately owned or state run?"

"The state protects individual enterprise," he replied.

Qiuju looked undecided, so he added, "This place may be small but it's clean. I always change the sheets. Come in and have a look around and see what you think." He was very friendly. She took a look and saw that the floors and beds were spotlessly clean. She decided to stay.

Having achieved his sale, the inn-keeper relaxed a little and began to chat. "Are you in town on urgent business?" he asked.

"To bring a case against someone," said Qiuju, and told him about her husband's injuries. "If I don't get this whole thing sorted out, we will have

harder times in the future," she told him. The inn-
keeper was sympathetic.

She waited anxiously for the police to start work
again and got to the police station at the same time as
two men in uniform who looked at the indictment and
the evidence and then at the doctor's diagnosis.

"Why is this from a hospital outside the province?"
they asked. She explained. The two men took out
their notebooks, asked her a few questions, wrote
down something and took her fingerprints. Then they
said, "You go on home. We will handle this. We've
got some urgent cases on our hands at the moment,
though, so you'll have to be a bit patient." The sun
shone into Qiuju's face as she left the building. It
made her nose itch so much that she sneezed. Suddenly she heard someone calling her. It was Li, the public
security man.

"What are you doing here?" he asked. "Did
Wang Changzhu give you the money?"

She gave no response.

"How dare he not pay?" he said, much surprised.

"It's not that he didn't pay. It's the way he paid
it."

"That Wang Changzhu really has no sense," said
the security man disapprovingly. "It's my fault, too.
We should have settled the whole thing face to face.
Then we wouldn't be in this mess."

"We've set our faces against each other," said
Qiuju. "Our sons and grandsons will be enemies
too."

"Some people just don't know what's good for
them," said Li. Seeing that he seemed to be on her
side, she explained: "I went to look for you but you

were away. So I came here. I've just handed in my indictment.''

"That is your right," said Li, sternly. Someone
called him. Qiuju saw that it was one of the men to
whom she had just given her indictment. He had just
washed his cup and now stood in the corridor talking
to Li.

"A woman has just left. She came about some business in your area."

"I know about the case," said Li. "When will
you send someone down there?"

"Who can we spare now?"

"You'll have to send someone. I'm quite familiar
with what's going on. One of the parties concerned is
the village head. They can't settle it face to
face," argued Li.

At that point, it occurred to Qiuju that she ought
not to be listening to their conversation, so she hurried
to the front gate.

A few moments later, Li came out to speak to her.

"Right," he said. "Come to my office in a few
days."

"How many days?" asked Qiuju. "Please be exact." Li gave her a date and the two of them parted.

When the day came, Li was out dealing with an emer-
gency case. Someone else had passed the ruling of the
county police station to her. Qiuju listened as the document was read to her. It still contained the original
three items: medical and convalescence expenses to be
covered along with a compensatory sum. The figures
were much the same as before. "I've been round in a
circle and now I'm back where I started," thought

Qiuju to herself. The man reading the document saw her dumbfounded look and told her that Li had left a message saying that if she did not approve, she was entitled to take her case to a higher authority. Qiuju said very little. She went home and brought out two feeder pigs, not yet fully fattened up, for sale at a market in Jiangsu. The money would fund another trip to town.

Back in town, Qiuju stayed at the same inn. She went to the city police station and applied for a reconsideration of her case. When she got back to the inn, the keeper tried to reassure her.

"Don't worry too much about all this. You're not busy this afternoon, go and have a walk in the park. Relax and cheer yourself up a bit."

Qiuju chatted with him about the park. She had heard that a lot of work had been done on it over the last few years and that there were now a small lake and a memorial temple in which there was a *nanmu* coffin with gold trimmings. She decided to take his advice and go for a stroll.

At the temple, she asked the entry price. It was three and a half yuan, which she reluctantly forked out. Inside was a very ordinary hall and some very ordinary stone statues of horses and people. As she walked around, she saw a stone turtle carrying a stone tablet, which was not new to her either. However, under the turtle's nose was a large incense burner, around which stood a crowd of excited people. When she got closer, she saw the burner was full of water instead of ash. The people were throwing coins into the water, most of which sank and formed a shining pile at the bottom. Only a few coins floated on the surface.

The corner was sheltered from the wind and was

slightly warmer than the rest of the temple. In the sunniest spot, an old man in religious costume sat at a table and, when requested, changed bank notes for coins. The crowd varied in age and included a group of colourfully dressed youths who cheered every time they threw in a coin. Before each throw they made a wish, hoping to be promoted at work, to have a decent house, a nice wife or become high officials: lots of ordinary questions. Qiuju watched this scene distractedly for some moments and then went over and changed a fifty-fen note into coins. She pushed her way through the crowd, grasping the handful of coins. Would she win or lose the case? One after another, the coins all sank. Someone in the crowd was rather worried for her and threw some coins in on her behalf: five out of five floated. Qiuju's heart floated too and she gazed thoughtfully into the burner. Suddenly there was a great commotion. It was one of the colourfully clad youths trying to find out if he would win at the mahjong table that evening. Only then did Qiuju realize that it was all just a game. She pulled herself together and walked off to see the tomb.

The tomb was in fact a cave cut into the hillside. Qiuju walked only forty or fifty paces, turned a corner and there was the coffin, directly in front of her. It was no bigger than coffins that she had seen before and the lacquer was chestnut-coloured: nothing out of the ordinary. It was not worth three and a half yuan.

She wandered back into the park. The gate looked familiar. But on crossing the little stone arched bridge, she saw that the original green-house full of flowers had been turned into an amusement centre. The wind was quite chilly. Two girls sat huddled in a ticket kiosk. There were very few visitors, only two couples with two children. The children were shouting for a ride on the "whirlwind". The parents went to buy tickets, but the two girls refused to sell them any. The two parties began to argue, "But we're from out of town. We've come a long way."

"It's too cold," said the girls, "and it's not Sunday; and anyway there are too few of you. We need a good twenty people to make it worth our while." The children made even more fuss.

"What if I buy twenty tickets?" asked an exasperated father.

Each ticket cost six yuan. The man handed the girl the money, who came out with her head inside her coat and started the machine. The man went over to Qiuju and offered her a free ride. She stepped reluctantly onto the "whirlwind" and had a good look at it. It was a metal plate with aeroplane-shaped seats. As soon as she sat down, the "whirlwind" began to move.

It was not quite what she had expected. Instead it was similar to riding a crazed mule or an angered cow or a sow whose piglet had been stolen; leaping around chaotically. Qiuju felt it more of a hardship than a pleasure. The land and sky kept changing places. The sky would fall diagonally and then suddenly jerk back up again. Sometimes the land followed the sky and sometimes the two became mixed together. Apart from that, her stomach was also playing at acrobatics. Her intestines, stomach, heart and lungs — all her vital internal organs — swung backwards and forwards. She was quite numb. Then her head began to spin and she felt quite dizzy, long after the "whirlwind" had stopped spinning. When she had calmed down, she saw the two couples standing on the ground looking up at the children who had climbed onto a high platform and were yelling that they wanted to go on another ride now. An official-looking gentleman arrived and called the children down. He asked one of the fathers: "Are you buying tickets?"

"No," said the man, "apparently it's too cold and there are too few of us."

"Who says?" asked the official-looking gentleman who then went and had words with the girls in the kiosk. The girls had no choice but to sell the tickets, but one of them called after the official, "It's all right for you, in a comfortable office all day. You should try working out here in the freezing cold!" Then she climbed up onto the high platform and switched the machine on.

This machine had rows of seats, two seats per row: for one adult and one child. It looked as if they were cycling along a rail in the sky. Qiuju thought it looked terribly dangerous, and left.

At the inn she said to the keeper, "I paid three and a half yuan to see nothing much and then nearly fainted for no charge at all." After a while, their conversation turned to the case.

"This may be a matter of enormous importance to you," said the inn-keeper, "but to anyone else it's really a very small matter. You're lucky that the police have time to deal with your case. These are days when policemen are greatly outnumbered by problems. The younger generation have no respect for tradition; they cheat and steal and want to kill someone over one angry word. I don't know..."

"So, do you think this is all for nothing?" asked Qiuju anxiously.

"No, no, not necessarily," he replied. Qiuju went to bed feeling rather downhearted.

She got up early the next morning. The inn-keeper told her, "I didn't tell you everything yesterday. Now I'll spill it all out. You appealed to the county police station last time. In fact the whole affair was handed by people lower down. The police chief merely glanced at the report and put his stamp on it. Now you appeal at the city level. The same thing will happen again. There are just too many cases and yours isn't particularly serious. You'll probably get the same decision with a different stamp on it. I reckon the best thing for you to do is to go and see the chief of police yourself. That way you might be able to make an impression on him."

"Right then, I'll go and see him," said Qiuju urgently.

"You don't understand," he said, "You probably won't be allowed into his office. Even if they do let you in, there'd be so many people wanting to speak to him that you wouldn't get a word in edgeways." She waited for him to finish. "Your best bet would be to casually ask his address and then go and find him one afternoon or evening."

Qiuju did not respond.

"I'm not telling you this for the sake of my business," continued the inn-keeper. "Another three yuan won't make me a rich man!"

"I'm just thinking," said Qiuju. "If everyone had the same idea and went knocking on the police chief's door, the poor man wouldn't get a moment's peace."

"Everyone will think what you're thinking, so very few people will actually go," said the inn-keeper craftily.

She went to the city police office and asked at reception for Yan Limin. The receptionist took a good look at her. "You're looking for Captain Yan?" she queried.

"Yes," said Qiuju, "I've come a long way to see him; from the country. If he's busy, I'll go to his house and wait for him there. He hasn't moved house, has he? Only I haven't been here for seven or eight years."

The receptionist told her, "Captain Yan isn't in his office. He was stabbed last night. He's probably still in hospital."

"Really?" said Qiuju. She was shocked.

The receptionist told her the details. "Last night there was a meeting at the station that went on until nearly midnight. By the time Captain Yan got home it was well past one o'clock. There was nothing on TV and he was tired so he started to get ready for bed. He'd just washed his feet and was about to throw the water away when he heard someone trying to prize open his front door. He flung the door open and frightened the burglar who stabbed at him with a knife. The captain dodged out of the way and the knife fell to the floor. The thief fled, but Captain Yan chased him and managed to grab hold of him. There were two more of them, though, both with knives. He managed to dodge one knife, but the other got him. Then they tried to run off, and in spite of the pain, the captain grabbed one and wouldn't let go. By then all his neighbours had rushed out and caught another. The last one leapt out of the window and injured his leg, so he couldn't escape." Qiuju listened to this and thought: Everything in this world is difficult. A police chief must be at greater risk than anyone else, what with criminals holding grudges. She assumed that that was the case with the three attackers. If Captain Yan had been asleep in bed who knows what might have happened to him and his family.

"How is he?" she inquired.

"Oh, it's not serious."

"I think I'll go and see him at home," decided Qiuju.

She followed the receptionist's directions to Captain Yan's home. She took two buses, walked about the length of a field, turned left into a narrow street, past a school and a row of buildings on one side, and on the other an unused patch of land and a pool of murky water. Beside the pool grew broad beans and other vegetables; around it was a rough fence made of branches. This all made up to five or six fields' distance and she turned right through a large gate. Inside was a large yard of uneven ground with lots of trees of different kinds and different sizes, and eight rows of grey buildings. She thought that the police captain probably lived in one of those. She asked someone who pointed to a red building among the trees on the slope. Eventually Qiuju found the correct building which faced east and had a width of about ten rooms and two storeys. She stood outside for a few minutes, memorizing the route she had taken. Then she turned around and went home.

When she arrived at the inn, the inn-keeper had already heard the news about the police chief and was full of gossip.

"At first everyone thought that they had a grudge against the captain and had come for revenge. But all three of them had Northwestern accents. It turned out that they'd fled from the Northwest after committing some crime or other and were only looking for a place to hide and an ordinary person to steal some money from before attempting a bigger job. They had no idea that they were breaking into the home of a police captain!"

"Didn't they know that the place was the police living quarters?" asked Qiuju.

"They didn't know what it was. They'd come a long way, remember. Besides, it's not just policemen who live there; there are people from other units too."

"Why doesn't Captain Yan live in special police housing?" she wondered aloud.

"He rejects his privilege and lives at his wife's work unit," replied the inn-keeper.

Qiuju looked enlightened. "Oh, I see," she said, "I thought it didn't look like the sort of place he'd live in."

"It's difficult to know what to do now," pondered the inn-keeper. "You can't very well go to the hospital empty-handed, but then again you can't give presents to police chiefs — that could be taken the wrong way." This gave Qiuju an idea.

That afternoon she went to a market down an old street about three or four *li* long. It was not a busy time for shoppers, but there was a vast range of things

to buy — all set out in good order: there were sec-
tions for selling vegetables, meat, poultry, livestock and
beancurd, for example. There were stalls selling expensive out-of-season fruits and vegetables such as cucum-
ber, aubergines, *huzi* (a type of edible gourd) and even
melons of different kinds apparently grown in local
greenhouses. Qiuju thought to herself: "You could
probably find peaches of immortality here if you
searched hard enough." The streetsellers themselves
varied nearly as much as their wares — some were old
men and women, others were only in their twenties:
girls with soft fair skin and pretty as dolls, elaborately
made-up but wearing greasy clothes, selling meat. They
stood by their stalls, shouting for customers in shrill
voices. Qiuju observed them all as she strolled past.
Walking and watching, she dawdled until the late-night
vendors selling fish put up their stalls. She stared into
a crate of live fish and picked out four, about five kilos
each. And four sounded like good luck. Having paid
for them and placed them in a bag, she set off by bus
on the complicated route to Captain Yan's house.
When she arrived at the red building, she walked
around the outside twice before finding the way in. The
sun was already setting and there was ice on the
ground which cracked under foot. She asked a child
for directions and was shown to the far door. She
knocked, but could hear no movement inside, so she
pushed it open and went in. Inside was a corridor as
wide as a water trench plus the length of a field. On
one side were windows which opened onto the outside,
on the other were front doors; one opposite each window. She counted along to the middle door and then
knocked. An old lady answered. It appeared that she

was alone in the house.

Though smiling, the old lady had an extremely irritating voice. It sounded as if she were permanently in the middle of a terrible argument. Qiuju offered her the fish tentatively, and the old lady accepted them.

"I'm from Wangqiao Village," said Qiuju urgently, "by the reservoir, northwest from here. Our village head is Wang Changzhu. My name is Qiuju. My husband is called Wan Shanqing. Would you mention me to Captain Yan please? He'll know who I am." With that she left and returned to the inn where she stayed one more night. Then she went home to wait for news.

Over the next couple of months, the swelling on her husband's leg reduced considerably and he was able to get up and walk around again. During this time Qiuju busied herself around the house and the fields. She still had some of the money that she had made from selling the two pigs and she used this to buy four piglets. She kept them in a sty and fed them on corn mixed with bran husks, intending to have them nicely fattened by springtime. She spread the mud from the pigsty and phosphate and fertilizer on the fields. By the time she had finished, it was already mid-February and Spring Festival had passed.

Wan Shanqing came out to the field to help his wife. He would become exhausted after only the slightest exertion.

"What's upsetting you?" asked Qiuju.

"My chest feels tight," he answered.

"You'll never get better with this depressing business hanging over us," complained Qiuju. "It's been a long time. We should have heard some news by now. I fear I'll have to go into town again."

"We had two successive heavy snows a fortnight ago. Even though there is nothing to do here in the fields, you shouldn't go now with the ground all frozen. It's going to snow soon. And the ferry is frozen up too. You'll exhaust yourself if you traipse through the snow all the way along the new road," warned her husband.

Qiuju said, "Officially, I've applied for a reconsideration; unofficially, I sent some fish. I really ought to have heard from Captain Yan by now."

"So many problems!" her husband sighed. "If we had just agreed to grow rape instead of wheat, we'd never have had this trouble."

Qiuju glared at him, "Is that really what you now think?"

"Well, it wasn't his own idea," protested her husband. "The order came from above: everyone was supposed to grow rape. He picked on us because our field is by the road to the village where everyone can see it. Everyone else has planted rape. It was only us who insisted on planting wheat. It's like the village head said: an ugly scab. Last time the officials came here, they took points off the score of the whole village. If you look at it like that, you could say we were somewhat in the wrong."

"Don't forget a few years ago he selected the very same spot to grow three seasons of rice because those higher-up said so. And the village elders could not dissuade him!" argued Qiuju. "He knew very well that it wouldn't be as profitable as growing rice and wheat alternately or rice and rape, but he insisted and the third crop was really poor.''

"That was ten years ago or more," her husband reasoned. "He had no choice but to follow instructions."

"Well, he was only chief of the militia battalion, the smallest potato. But he would go out of his way to tread on others in order to climb up. Times are different now; he has no right to beat someone whenever he feels like it, not to say kicking you in your vital parts."

In the middle of this argument, someone shouted from the rape field, "Wan Shanqing! The village head wants to see you at his house."

"Let me go," said Qiuju.

"Don't go to extremes," said her husband.

"But I've already reported him and applied for a reconsideration."

"Don't press him too hard. If he doesn't give a formal apology, accept an informal one," said the husband.

Qiuju nodded in agreement and walked disconsolately back to the village. As usual, when she got to the village head's house she gave the dog a wide berth. From inside the house came much shouting and she assumed that he had guests from the government. She peered in but saw only familiar faces from the village. On noticing her, he stood up and came to the door.

"You've come then?"

"Yes."

He smiled and said, "I've set out the mahjong tables."

"What's that got to do with me?" she asked.

The village head's smile disappeared.

"Aren't you always visiting the police station and law courts? You've already complained to the town, county and city police. You have a strong background in making accusations: I'm here gambling — aren't you going to report me?"

His voice was heard by the people inside.

A few guests who had been watching the game suddenly looked up at him.

"Did you send for me just to insult me? Do you think I'm afraid to go back to the police?" Qiuju replied indignantly.

"I haven't finished," sneered the village head, but she was no longer listening. She hurried away, holding her breath.

After a while the clouds became thicker and the wind died down. The incident had so infuriated her that she sweated with the effort of trudging along the road. She came to the quayside and looked over the billowing water.

She waited on the shore — there were no boats.

She knocked on the boatman's door; he was sitting inside by the stove, warming himself.

"The ice in the middle has already melted but there's still a lot around the edges," he said. "It melts a little in the day, but freezes again at night. The boat just can't be taken out in these conditions."

He got up and pointed towards the reservoir. At the door the boatman shivered and leaned against the door frame.

"Look at the clouds — it's going to snow again soon. I'm afraid I won't be able to cross the reservoir until after the snow."

Qiuju told him her predicament.

"The village head has deliberately made you angry — by the time you return with a policeman, all the mahjong blocks and money will be well hidden. You don't even know if he really is gambling. Ignore him. Go home and rest."

At home, her husband asked her, "Where have you been? When I got back from the fields, the village head came over. He said that you left without hearing him out. The reconsideration certificate from the city police has already arrived — it's the same as the last one."

Qiuju was dumbfounded. She looked at the red stamp on the sheet of paper and sat down quietly. Then she said, "He's the head of the village and defendant in this case — he shouldn't be the one to pass this on to us. I'll have to go into town and find out what's going on."

Her husband stopped her. "How are you going to get there? You can't cross the river."

"I'll take the new road."

"But that's miles out of your way — look at the weather."

Outside snowflakes floated in the air.

Qiuju walked out of the village. It was already snowing heavily as she began to walk along the new road. As she got nearer Jiangsu Province, the snow was falling thick and fast like cotton wool, shattering into pieces as it hit the ground. Everything around her was covered with a blanket of white.

Snowflakes danced before her eyes. The old snow had already been trodden by a thousand feet and was packed solid. This was now covered with a sticky, slippery new layer. Struggling through the bitter weather, Qiuju cursed the gods for her hard life and resolved to overcome her difficulties.

It was dark when she arrived in the town, so she went straight to the same inn. The following day, she changed into a different outfit and proceeded to the police station.

The same receptionist pointed out the way to her and said, "Captain Yan is in his office; I think he's free at the moment." She went in and saw a middle-aged man sitting at a desk.

"Captain Yan, I presume?" she asked and then explained, 'I'm from Wangqiao Village, Xibei Township. Our village head is called Wang Changzhu. My name is Qiuju, my husband is Wan Shanqing."

She then told him her story.

"You mean you know nothing about this?" she concluded in surprise. Captain Yan spoke while making her some tea, "There are several captains, each with a different area of work. Captain Wang is in charge of this kind of problem, but he's not here at the moment. I'll find someone to help you."

"I came especially to find you," she said urgently. "I went to your house the day after you were injured by that thief. You were in hospital but an old lady received me."

"Oh yes, she's a relative from up north. She's rather deaf and always talks as if she were quarelling. Did she frighten you?"

When she heard this, Qiuju suspected that the old lady had not understood what she had said to her that day, and so Captain Yan probably did not know about the fish. That was money down the drain, because she felt that she couldn't really tell him now. She just said, "I made a complaint about my village head and your office gave him a report to pass on to me. This is surely not the correct procedure."

Captain Yan listened to her and then went through to another room. Qiuju looked around her at the furniture. It was simple and rather shabby. By her side was a sofa, on the wall above her head was some calligraphy. In the centre of the room was a stove with an iron chimney to carry the smoke out of the window. In front of the stove was a table about four times the standard size, and a swivel chair. Behind that, a waste bin full of balls of screwed-up paper. On the table was a stone slab with two pens sticking on it; two bottles of ink; some paper in a wire tray and a narrow-waisted teacup just like the ones she had seen Li and the others use. Captain Yan returned and said, "Wait a moment, I've sent someone to inquire about this matter." In a couple of minutes, they were joined by a third voice.

"I've just made a phone call. A Comrade Li is in charge of this case. He said that originally he wanted to take the report to the village himself, but he had to deal with another case about a stolen cow, so his secretary went instead. Due to bad weather conditions, the secretary couldn't cross the reservoir and was making preparations to take the new road when he bumped into Village Head Wang. The secretary was new and didn't realize that this man was the defendant, so asked him to take the report to the village for him."

"Well, if that's the case, I can't blame you," said Qiuju.

"What do you think about the latest decision?'' Captain Yan asked her.

"I am just an ordinary person and he's the head of the village. First I went to Li at the township and then to the county police and finally to the city police. I got the same result every time. What can I do?" she asked.

Captain Yan replied: "We're not immune to errors. Our powers are limited. If you're not happy, you can take him to court. That's your right."

"How should I set about that?" Qiuju asked.

Yan said, "In this situation, you should get a lawyer."

Qiuju guessed by the tone of his voice that he had not been told about the case at all; only now did she realize that she had been taking a circuitous path to getting justice done. With this thought, she seized the opportunity to ask, "I don't know any lawyers. Can you introduce me to one?"

Captain Yan wrote down a name and gave it to her, saying, "Go to the Justice Department and ask for this person." The name was Wu, the lawyer she had met before. When she saw him again, he praised her:

"You already understand the use of the new law — Excellent!"

Confused, she replied: "I don't know about any new law. I only need to know whether I can win this case."

"I know nothing about this case," he told her. "It's hard to say — do you need an attorney?"

"What about the fees, would they be the same as before?"

Lawyer Wu frowned. "Of course."

"Oh well, I won't bother then, but would you help

me to write an official complaint?''

She went to the law courts to hand in the complaint, and when she walked back onto the street, the snow had thinned to rain. She went back to the inn and chatted to the keeper for a while before sleeping. The next day, she waded back home along the wet roads in her muddy clothes.

The fields gradually thawed back into life as the days grew warmer. The rape blossomed like a golden lake surrounding an island of wheat in its centre. The animals became restless, and Qiuju's four piglets seemed to have doubled in size, snorting and snuffling in their sty.

Her husband was noticeably better, except for the impending case that hung over him like a shadow.

By the time the court had issued a summons, the inn prices had increased; the keeper only charged her fifty fen extra out of kindness and sympathy for her.

"At the beginning of the year, the government declared a law by which citizens can bring cases against officials. At first, people thought they were only going through the motions, but I've heard that a peasant woman has made a case against the city police office. She is the first person to do that and the famous Captain Yan will be at court to represent the police.''

Qiuju said dubiously, "Perhaps she's eaten too much fat and it's gone to her head. How can she possibly win?''

"The case has shaken the whole city and the surrounding villages. Everyone wants to know the result. The hotels are jammed with reporters,'' the inn-keeper said.

"Have they come to laugh at the stupid peasant?" she asked.

"You don't understand — the government has made this new law and no-one really knows what it is all about. The government wants everyone to understand how it works, so they will select an important case and deal with it very carefully so that everyone can see for himself and fully understand."

"Do you think the peasant woman will win?" she asked again.

"If she fails the new law will fail too — no one would ever use it again."

"The world is really out of order," said Qiuju. "If the ordinary citizen is wrong, and the government is right, would the government still declare itself in the wrong?"

"They'll have to judge it according to facts, of course," the inn-keeper answered. "But this is the first time the law has been used and the case is special — this case was chosen because the woman was in the right. Anyway, this is not a very big case. When the peasant wins, it will not be a terrible embarrassment to the government and will also show how tolerant and lenient it can be."

This news filled Qiuju's head that night as she made ready for bed.

The next day the sun shone brightly and everything looked clear and colourful. The ground soaked by the rain of several days had nearly dried out and the moist warm air was a pleasure to breathe. The people in the streets looked refreshed, there was a spring in their steps and they shouted joyfully. Street stalls offered opportunities to buy everything from food to daily necessities and stallholders shouted their wares like a forest full of birds.

It was as if the whole city was washed and glowing with health.

Qiuju took the summons to the courts and saw downstairs that the courtyard was full of people. From their faces it was obvious that they had something serious on their minds, but their chatter was casual. She went over to a group to listen to what was being said. She saw the inn-keeper talking with another group and asked him, "Who's looking after the inn?"

"The case I told you of yesterday goes to court today," he said. "It will be the chance of a lifetime. Never mind about the inn."

Qiuju suddenly felt suspicious. "How many cases does the court handle each day?" she asked.

"It varies, sometimes none at all for several days. Sometimes several cases in one day, sometimes one case takes several days. But this morning there is just one case."

Qiuju was about to speak again when the inn-keeper waved his hand, saying, "A friend of mine is reserving a seat for me. Soon it'll be so crowded that we won't be able to get in through the door."

She heard someone call her. It was a bailiff whom she had seen before.

"There you are," he said. "We've been looking for you everywhere."

"I was told it would start at 9:00. There's still more than ten minutes."

"The court session starts at 9:00 on the dot. You should be here at least ten minutes in advance."

Qiuju looked anxious.

"Do you want to go to the ladies?" he asked. "Upstairs on the left. Don't worry, I'll wait for you here."

When she came back downstairs she followed the bailiff through a small door and across a room with tables and chairs, then through another door into the courtroom.

Entering, she felt the gaze of many pairs of eyes following her movements. The pressure of their gaze forced her to bow her head. She was led across a platform and down five or six steps, and after a few more paces she stood by the semi-circular stand. She sat down behind it while the bailiff moved away.

The room was filled with the hum of many voices speaking simultaneously. She gradually calmed herself and looked around the courtroom. It was set on an incline, with the judge's chair higher than the rest. The spectator seating was also sloped so that those on seats at the back were positioned higher than those at the front, to enable everyone to get a good view. All the seats were occupied. The corridors and doorways were also packed with people. Perhaps they had just arrived, she thought, or possibly all the seats were already occupied.

In the midst of these confused thoughts came a muffled sound and everyone fell silent immediately. The people present all held their breath, as if waiting for a pin to drop. The judge entered and sat at the highest desk. He cleared his throat and said, "Today we shall hear the case of Qiuju versus the city police."

He then introduced the people taking part in the proceedings, beginning with himself and the two assessors sitting beside him, and a clerk at the side. At last he came to the plaintiff and called out her name. Qiuju stood up and answered. Then he called out the defendant's name. Someone in the opposite stand stood up and answered. When Qiuju looked up, the sun was streaming in through the courtroom window. The man standing opposite her was none other than Captain Yan of the city police. Qiuju was amazed. She heard the judge saying, "We shall first hear the report. As the plaintiff does not read very well, a court representative will read it on her behalf."

The court clerk had just read the first paragraph when Qiuju shouted, "This isn't right!" The audience began to mutter about the interruption but the judge tapped his gavel on the desk and they fell silent. He asked, "Plaintiff Qiuju, what do you want to say? Speak slowly and clearly. There is no need to hurry."

She said, "You've got it all wrong. The person I want to bring a case against is Wang Changzhu, head of Wangqiao Village, not Captain Yan."

"It's the same thing," said the judge kindly.

"How can it be the same?" she protested. "Captain Yan lives in the city; I live in the countryside. It's nothing to do with him. He's never even set eyes on my husband. How could I bring a case against him?"

The judge tried to explain, but Qiuju was anxious and impatient.

"I can't make head or tail of what you are saying. I just want to see Wang Changzhu, the man who beat my husband, over there in the defendant's box." More murmurs came from the audience until Captain Yan asked to speak and made a suggestion. The judge then whispered to his assessors who nodded their heads in agreement. He cleared his throat and said, "Court is adjourned." The people on the platform then stood up together and filed out through a door at the back of the courtroom. The bailiff led Qiuju away. Someone in the audience wondered aloud, "Is that all for this morning?" At which a uniformed clerk came in and said, "Court is ajourned for approximately half an hour."

Qiuju was led into the room where the judge and Captain Yan and some other people were sitting. She sat down and the bailiff poured her some tea. She noticed that all of them drank from narrow-waisted cups. The judge said to her, "Comrade Qiuju, we do apologize; we should have explained things to you beforehand."

She said reproachfully, "I really don't understand. I've been to the township, county and city police stations. Although they made mistakes, at least they were excusable mistakes. But you've got me prosecuting Captain Yan. You've really made me put my fingers in the fire."

The judge, not knowing quite what to say, laughed. Captain Yan and the others laughed too.

"How can you laugh, Captain Yan?" asked Qiuju incredulously. "They're making me prosecute you."

Someone interrupted her. "Defendant is only a term," he said. "In civil and administrative cases, the 'defendant' is not necessarily on trial as an individual."

Captain Yan explained: "The village head beat your husband. That should have been dealt with by the local police. The township police made a decision with which you didn't agree, so you applied to the city po-

lice for reconsideration. You didn't agree with their decision either, so you brought the case to court. That is
your legal right. You are representing your side and I
am representing the city police office and defending
their decision. You and I have equal rights and it's up
to the court to decide whether the city police acted
correctly or not." He gestured to Qiuju to drink her
tea. She took a few sips and then asked, "Well, what
if the court decides you're in the wrong?"

"We would have to punish Wang Changzhu according to the court's decision." Everyone nodded in
agreement and drank their tea.

Qiuju went upstairs to the toilet and then followed
the judge and the other officials back into the
courtroom. This time the atmosphere was better and
she felt a little more relaxed. The court bell rang and
everyone fell silent. Clearing his throat, the judge began
his introductions all over again. When he had finished,
the clerk read out the charges. The report was clear
and to the point and the clerk read it articulately. Then
the defendant read out his reply to the charges. Captain Yan spoke first, followed by the people beside him
who added a few words. They simply explained how
the county police had made their decision: which
clauses of which laws they had used, how the city police had reconsidered the case. It all sounded very reasonable. The audience could not help commenting a little to each other, but they stopped as soon as someone spoke again. When both sides had finished, the
judge asked a few more questions and let the two parties argue a while; and then, when everything that
needed to be said had been said, he announced:
"Court is ajourned for this morning. We shall

reconvene at 4 pm.''

The audience dispersed. The judge came over to Qiuju and said, "It's not easy for you to come all the way into town. Although the views expressed this morning were contradictory, everyone is agreed about the facts and we have all the proofs too. We'll work through lunch so that we can come to a decision by four o'clock.'' She thanked him and left.

She had lunch at a stall on her way back. At the inn, the keeper was waiting at the window. He praised her performance and talked about the afternoon's decision.

"There seems to be no disagreement about the fact,'' he said, "but both the county police and the city police had good reasons behind their decisions.''

"You mean I'll lose?'' asked Qiuju in disappointment.

"You must win! It's like I said yesterday: The government wants to make an example of this case so as to make an impression on people. The court will certainly decide in your favour.'' This set Qiuju's mind at rest. "Don't worry,'' continued the inn-keeper, "go out for a walk this afternoon.''

She rested for a while and then strolled to the lake by the old city wall. She noticed that the tree groves which she had seen seven or eight years before had been pruned and now new trees had been planted; some tall, some short, some she recognized, some she had not seen before. "They'll be beautiful in summer,'' she thought to herself. She saw trees with purple leaves __ a colour that reminded her of cold pig's blood. Looking back after walking some distance, she thought they looked like Chinese roses.

Among the trees were lots of stone animals she was familiar with: a lion springing into attack; an elephant
with its trunk in the air; a running ostrich; a sleeping
bear; and two animals that she felt should not be put
together, a tiger on top of a horse. The tiger had its
teeth in the horse — not a pleasant sight. Dotted
around and across the water were several pavilions and
bridges. No two pavilions were the same. Some with
one storey, some with two or three, some beside the
roads, others beside bridges. The bridges varied too:
arched, zigzagged, or ordinary ones. Nothing unusual.
The water was not as clear as it had been seven or
eight years ago.

Suddenly she heard an uproar. She turned a corner
and saw that the place where the lake curved in was
paved with stone, about half the size of a field. In the
warm sun stood a group of colourfully dressed people
taking off their clothes — men and women together.
None of them looked embarrassed despite the fact that
they all had next to nothing on underneath. The men
were wearing nothing but a small piece of thin cloth;
the women were either in one-piece or two-piece costumes, much like underwear. They ran around the
coves, took a deep breath and leapt into the cold water.
Many a wet head was visible in the water. Men
and women in a pavilion further away were jumping
into the water one after another. Watching them, Qiuju
felt so cold that goose pimples appeared on her arms.
She unconsciously withdrew a few paces and stood
among the trees on the slope, where she encountered
another group of people. They obviously had nothing
to do with the swimmers as they were all wrapped up
warmly in plenty of clothes — jumpers, cotton pad-

ding, and down coats. Some folded their arms inside
their sleeves; others thrust their hands deep into their
pockets. They were all gazing down at the scantily-clad
swimmers, most of whom were teenage girls in red,
green, yellow and purple costumes, playing animatedly
in the water. When the girls climbed out onto the
shore, they were in no hurry to get dressed. Instead
they stood still and allowed the water to drip from
their bodies and evaporate in the sun. Then the wind
blew across the cove and they all shivered and dried
themselves and picked up their clothes. The spectators
next to Qiuju were paying particular attention to a girl
in red who had made no effort to find a private place
in which to dress herself and stood in full view of everyone as she changed her clothes. She put a towel
around her waist, bent and quickly took off her wet
clothes underneath and put on dry ones. At the same
time she continued chatting with the men around her.
She pulled a shirt over her head and tried to pull off
her wet top from underneath that. She struggled at
first; perhaps one of the buttons would not come
undone or the strap had become twisted. When she
eventually yanked it away, two white breasts flitted
under her shirt. The spectators on the bank gaped but
the girl carried on chatting. When these people were all
dressed, the audience turned their attention back to the
swimmers.

The sun was now setting. Qiuju asked someone the
time and then turned around and went directly back to
the courthouse.

At four o'clock sharp the courthouse bell rang. The
judge summarized the morning's proceedings, stood
up and clearing his throat, announced the decision,

"This case has been carefully discussed and considered according to law. We have now come to the following conclusion: The decision of the city police on the decision of the county police about Wang Changzhu, head of Wangqiao Village, is quite correct. We have no objection."

Qiuju realized that she had lost the case. In her stupor she could hear sympathetic murmurs from the audience, already on its way out. Captain Yan and a few others came over to commiserate with her. They said that if she still had any objections, she had the right to appeal to a higher court. That raised her hopes, "Definitely," she said. "Appeal! Definitely…"

Two months after her appeal, the weather was becoming warmer and warmer. The leaves turned deep green; the whole earth became green. The rape plants shed their flowers and grew pods, the wheat stood up straight in the fields. The four piglets grew even bigger and would soon be large enough to sell.

One day Qiuju was spreading fertilizer on the fields. She had not completed two furrows when someone told her that a government official had arrived.

"Do they want me to go to the village head's house?"

The messenger said, "No, to the village hall. Three people have come and the village head has gone to see them; when he left his face looked quite different. It was as if someone had just asked him to repay a big loan."

Qiuju put her tools away and went to the village hall. The official's car was outside — white with two blue stripes along the side and a red light on top — it was a police car. As she got closer, she could hear voices from inside the building; they were talking about her. She slowed her pace and listened.

She heard a stranger's voice say, "This woman has reported to the township, county and city police, then to the county court and now to us at the middle-level court. At first, I thought she was a shrew. Now, after holding several meetings and investigations, everyone has come to the conclusion that she's a good woman." Another voice, older than the first, said, "The previous punishment was lawful, commensurate with the man's injuries and the way he was beaten up. Qiuju is not a trouble-maker and she's not crazy either. Why hasn't she given up? Maybe she has a reason?"

A third person said, "It's not easy for you to come to the village. Why not listen carefully to what she has to say."

The voice sounded familiar, and she recognized it as Li's. Having reached the door already, there was no turning back now. She walked with heavier footsteps and the voices stopped at the sound of her approach. She saw Li and two other uniformed men sitting inside. Li introduced them.

"These two gentlemen from the mid-level courts are in charge of your case. Judicial officers Zhu and Yang."

All three were drinking from narrow-waisted teacups. Li rose to make her some tea, but she preferred to do it herself, filling the others' cups at the same time.

The older voice was Zhu's whilst the young one was Yang's. The two requested her to tell them her story in detail from beginning to end.

Qiuju cleared her thoughts and began.

"After the autumn harvest, the village head decided that the whole village should grow rape __ that's how it started. In fact, it was an order from the government that we should plant the rape in a large plot, which everyone except us seemed to think was a good thing. He had chosen a plot by the road for the benefit of the government officials who would see it the instant they arrived. Not only was it a matter of the village head's personal reputation but of the 'face' of the whole village. As a result, everyone consented. Our land is three *mu*, situated in the middle of everyone else's land. Last year, we grew rape so this year we naturally had to grow something else, for the sake of the soil. We decided to grow wheat. At first the village head gave no indication of any disapproval so we carried on and planted the wheat. Even when the wheat was sprouting he said nothing; but then some officials came and docked points from the village. The village head was furious. Though we promised to grow rape next year, he ordered us to destroy all our crop and plant rape instead. How could we get rid of a field full of crops? Angry words were exchanged and the village head hit my husband."

Zhu and Yang wrote all this down in their notebooks. Then they said, "Tell us exactly how your husband was hit."

Qiuju explained: "He's the village head, in charge of everyone in the village. It's like a big family; the parent can give orders to his children or beat and curse them. But he! He kicked my husband in the chest and his private parts. It was really dangerous —— could have been fatal!"

Yang interrupted her to ask: "The investigation papers only said that your husband had been kicked lower down — there was nothing about any chest injuries."

Qiuju said, "Lots of people saw what happened. I'm not making it up. That injury was not bad enough to need the doctor's attention so I didn't bother to write it down."

Zhu asked, "You say that your husband feels pressure in his chest after only a short period of work?"

"My husband was beaten up — could it be any more serious? I took my case to all those places before I got to you. So far I haven't managed to get it properly settled. He's injured and angry. It's not surprising that he finds it difficult to work, is it?"

Having listened to her speech, the two officials looked at each other, exchanged a few words and then asked, "Is your husband at home at the moment?"

"He's working in the fields."

"Right, let's go and see him."

The sun shone from a cloudless sky as they walked out of the village. Fields stretched as far as the eye could see while weeds that had been allowed to grow unchecked on the paths rustled underfoot as they walked. She led the three men to her husband. He had just finished fertilizing another two furrows and now stood resting on his spade. Qiuju introduced them, and after a brief chat her husband removed his shirt and showed the officials his injuries.

"Do you have any X-rays from the hospital?" they asked.

Qiuju replied: "If you wait until this evening, we'll have enough time to go to the hospital in Jiangsu.

We'll return as soon as possible."

Li said, "The district hospital? Last time, as it was a special case, we accepted their evidence. But according to the law, only reports from the county hospital or higher are valid."

Qiuju said awkwardly: "We're rather busy in the fields at the moment, so we haven't got much time to go into town. And it's so difficult..."

"We'll give you a lift into town," the officials offered. Qiuju was about to reply when she realized that lots of people were watching them. This worried her and she said, "Thank you for the offer, but this is a very small place and rumours spread easily. Everyone knows that police cars are for criminals to ride in — tongues wouldn't stop wagging." The three men did not know what to suggest.

Qiuju asked, "What about if my husband and I go by ferry and meet you in town and then go to the hospital together?" They agreed and set off down the new road.

In town, having had the X-rays taken, they stayed at the same inn. The keeper inquired as to how they were. Qiuju said, "Look, although it doesn't seem he had been kicked very hard it was hard enough to break one of his ribs. The doctor said that it isn't healing properly __ which is why there's permanent pressure on his chest."

The inn-keeper asked whether they had got a medical certificate. She replied:

"Yes, the doctor said it was a 'mild injury'. Last time he said it was 'very mild'."

The inn-keeper nodded and said, "Three years ago a similar thing happened to a relative of mine; he also went to court, so I know a little about this sort of thing. So the nature of the injury is different now." At her request he continued:

"'Very mild injury', 'mild injury' and 'serious injury' are all different. The first is when only the skin or muscles are damaged; the second and third are injuries to bones and tendons, but their degrees are different. For example, if three or four of your ribs or your leg or wrist are broken, they're a 'mild injury'. But when an internal organ or an eye or ear is injured, they're classed as 'serious injuries'." Rather confused, Qiuju asked, "But if you're injured in the hand or foot it could stop you working. Ears are useless — if you lose one you can carry on as before. Why does that count as a 'serious injury'?"

The inn-keeper said, "It's because it alters a person's appearance."

Qiuju asked, "Do the three types of injury result in different punishments?"

The inn-keeper replied: "The first is just a fine, while the last, as it is the most serious, could get the offender a life sentence. It's hard to say what they do about middle cases like yours. The offender could just get a short spell or one year in prison."

Qiuju said, "Do you think I'll win?"

"I'm really not sure — I got it wrong last time!"

Suddenly she noticed that the inn-keeper was holding a narrow-waisted cup, so she asked in surprise: "You also use that type of cup?"

"What about it?" asked the inn-keeper, rather bewildered.

Qiuju said, "Wherever I've been for this case, I've seen people using narrow-waisted cups: Li the public security person; the receptionist; Captain Yan; the judge and the judicial officers — everyone! I thought it must be part of the uniform for government officials."

The inn-keeper couldn't help laughing. "No, no, not at all. Autumn Pear tonic for coughs comes in this bottle. Many people get coughs; once they've finished the medicine, they keep the bottle and use it as a teacup. They've become quite popular in the city. Some perfectly healthy young people take advantage of free medical care and get the medicine on prescription. They throw the contents away to make cups. A friend gave me mine."

Qiuju and her husband both laughed. The inn-keeper smiled and said, "Your husband doesn't say much, does he?"

She said, "He's like a gourd without a hole."

"Although the doctor said he doesn't have to have the rib reset if he doesn't want to, you still need to think it over carefully," said the inn-keeper. "Office workers who do nothing but drink tea and read magazines all day don't really need to. But your husband labours in the fields and that could make the injury worse instead of better. Then again, if you have the operation, you've got to let them open up your chest."

"Yes, you're right," said Qiuju thoughtfully.

The inn-keeper said, "I've an old friend who's a retired doctor of Chinese medicine. His family have been doctors for generations. He'll be able to give you some medicine to sort it out. Would you have time to see him?"

She replied, "We can get some relatives to take care of the house. As for the fields, at the moment we could be busy twenty-four hours a day but nothing is really urgent."

"It's all settled then. You stay here for a few days and take some medicine; you can take the rest back home with you. I'm sure it will be effective."

Qiuju said, "We're waiting for the results of our court case. Should we inform the court that we're staying here instead of at home?"

The inn-keeper said, "There's no need, they're very busy so they probably won't get round to your case for at least a couple of weeks." she nodded.

"I'm not after your money," he said, "but prices have gone up again. Still, as we're good friends, you can stay for just three and a half yuan a night."

Qiuju and her husband stayed for about two weeks. The doctor did have some excellent methods. Not only did he cure Wan Shanqing's broken rib, he also made him feel much healthier in general. Qiuju and her husband thanked the doctor and the inn-keeper and then went home.

They got off the bus and walked towards the reservoir amid fields green with paddy seedlings and soon they covered the ten or twenty *li* distance to the ferry. Nobody was waiting at the quay. Qiuju and her husband stood and waited alone. Her husband was as quiet as ever, but she was used to his silence and ignored it. The wind blew over the water, which undulated gently, and through their clothes and onto their skin. Their vision seemed to ripple with the water. They watched the water rise suddenly and surge onto the shore, soaking the earth. The water looked quite different now that it was spring; it was a gorgeous azure blue. The grass on the bank, well trodden by many feet, had begun to sprout again. Overhead, the sun looked as if it had been freshly washed in the azure water and now shone clearly, giving the sky an opaque glow. The ground was misted over. Qiuju and her husband could not distinguish people from animals, or trees from crops on the other side of the water. The effort of gazing across the reservoir tired their eyes, so instead they watched the waves hitting a breakwater; and tried to decide whether the birds they could see were gulls or ducks. She saw how the reservoir narrowed and branched and eventually split into many smaller branches that carried the water onto the fields… Suddenly, she became aware that no-one was waiting for the ferry on the other side either; and there was no sign of the boatman, only a lone boat floating beside the shore. She cried out. Her shout, like her vision, reached the other shore indistinctly. Then her husband shouted together with her. Someone on the other side answered their call. She saw the boatman in the distance, holding a punting pole and pushing an empty boat out towards them. In the middle of the reservoir, he swapped the pole for oars. Not bothering to swap back, he rowed the rest of the way over to them. When he got to the shore, the boatman's expression seemed different from usual.

"I've had no customers for a few days now," he said. "I didn't expect you two today; I thought I'd stay in bed again."

"Where is everyone?" asked Qiuju, looking rather puzzled.

"The new road is complete now," said the boatman. "People would rather ride their bikes the long way round than take the ferry. Those who don't have a bike hitch a lift.''

"Haven't any outsiders been to the village?" she asked.

"People rarely want to come to this out-of-the-way place. If the government sends people, they come by car," said the boatman. "Two groups came this morning; a small van full of officials to check on the crops and another car. They both came along the new road." Then he said, rather sadly: "I'm afraid my boat and I are like old clothes put away in a trunk to rot.''

She could see how reluctant he was to part with his boat and sympathized with him. She searched for something to say but only came up with, "What did the other car come for?''

"I don't know," replied the boatman. He looked more carefully at Qiuju and recognized her. "Oh, you're from the Wan family, aren't you? Is this your husband? Have you got the result yet?''

"No, not yet," she replied. By this time, they had reached the shore.

When they arrived home, their relative who had been looking after their house said, "A police car came this morning and took the village head away." Qiuju could not believe it.

"Impossible," she said. "You must have got it wrong!''

"I was feeding the pigs when they arrived," said the relative, "so I didn't know what was going on at first. Then, when I heard a lot of voices outside, I ran out to see what was going on. I saw the village head coming out of his house with a uniformed officer on either side. At first I thought he was on his way to do some official business but then he tripped up slightly and the sun reflected off something metal. Everyone realized then that he was handcuffed.''

Qiuju was amazed. "Have any officials been to our house?'' she asked.

"No, no one,'' was the reply.

She thought for a while, still amazed, then she blurted out: "I only wanted an apology, not a prison sentence.''

Not knowing quite what to think or say, she busied herself cooking a meal. When she ate, the food seemed to have no flavour.

After lunch the relative said, "The wheat has gone bad. It's covered in black; it's a disease called 'smut', apparently.''

Qiuju and her husband rushed out to their field to look at the damage. It was not a happy scene. The surrounding rape plants had already been cut down and rice seedlings planted. They were already turning pale green in stark contrast with the dark, unhealthy colour of the wheat field. The wheat was waist-high and covered in black.

At the edge of the field, and again in the middle, Qiuju picked a couple of heads of wheat. She rolled them between her hands and blew away the chaff. Then she looked closely at the kernels and gauged their weight, trying to estimate the extent of the disease. She decided that sixty to eighty per cent was salvageable. She urged her husband to go on home as he must be tired. He refused. At that moment, she saw a crowd of people come towards them from the direction of the paddy field. They stopped in front of Qiuju and her husband, and one of them pointed to the wheat and said, "Let this be a lesson to you! We shall have to hold a big meeting in the village with all the village officials present." She recognized the speaker as a government agricultural expert who had come to the village to check the crops. Some years before he had come to teach them a method of planting without ploughing. She said to him, "I did everything you taught us. How could it all go so wrong?"

The agricultural expert looked around him and said, "Rape plants are harvested much earlier than wheat. When rice seedlings are planted afterwards, they are heavily watered and the water seeps into the wheat field. Young wheat an inch high can take lots of water, but when it grows taller, even an inch of water is enough to drown it. I said many times at lots of meetings that rape must only be grown on its own. Didn't your village head tell you?"

"Huh," said Qiuju, "he only suggested that we all grow rape and then, later on, he tried to force us to destroy our wheat and plant rape instead. If he had told us about the watering problem a little earlier, we could have avoided all this trouble."

There was nothing more to say. The crowd stood around for a while and then left in dribs and drabs. Her husband still refused to go home and rest, so Qiuju picked up her tools and went home on her own.

Translated by Anna Walling

Celestial River

I had seen my cousin three times altogether. This was the third time. It was the middle of the night.

There were only two people in the three-room apartment: she and I. A fourteen-square-metre room with a balcony separated the two of us. Next door to that room was the study. In the study there was a large writing desk, on top of which were an adjustable desk lamp, a galloping porcelain horse with a flowing mane, and two writing brushes. There were two bottles of ink: blue and black. There was a stack of writing paper. In front of the desk was a revolving chair. Against the wall were several bookcases, and each bookcase had seven or eight shelves, all filled neatly with books both thick and thin. There was also a bed with a light yellow mattress, red satin sheets and a white cotton quilt. Tonight my cousin was sleeping on that bed. It was my bed. For many years I had slept on that bed, but tonight it belonged to another person — my cousin.

I was separated from my cousin by a distance of one room. I could not decide whether or not to walk back to my room, to my bed.

Outside my window the evening had deepened into darkness and the sounds of nature were at last still. Perhaps I and the other person in the apartment were the last remaining living creatures on earth. I knew that at this hour we would not be disturbed: the apartment had an iron door and a chain lock.

I drank a cup of tea and smoked a cigarette. Curls of smoke floated upward past my eyes. I guessed that my indecisiveness must appear pretty stupid.

Thirty-two years ago there was a thirty-two year old man who had also injudiciously hesitated. As his recently pregnant wife had not yet been transferred so that they could live together, he sat alone in the three-bedroom apartment; it was impossible not to feel cold and lonely. He decided to go over to the bookcase to pull out a book. The seven or eight shelves on each of the bookcases against the wall were full. But it was not his study, it was the library room of his work place. He held a post in the secretariat of the provincial government.

Afterwards he had come here. It was a small red building with unique architecture and a spiral staircase. When he walked in the door, the books on the shelves seemed to callously draw him over. The reading room was still and empty. He pulled out a "Newspaper Reading Manual" and casually opened it at a page in full-colour showing pictures of flags of the world's nations. He sat and slowly scanned them. Another person entered. This person pulled out a book and sat opposite him. This man was his direct superior, the secretary-general of the province. The two men put aside their books and began chatting. The secretary-general said that the motion to promote him to head of the vice-secretariat had already been mentioned at the meeting. If there was little resistance to the move, it would be officially announced in two or three days. It was not news. He listened calmly to the secretary-general, inwardly ascertaining from the use of the word "resistance" the secretary-general's intention. He waited.

The secretary-general said: "The movement is spreading like a raging fire. Everyone is vying with one another, but you ... what is the matter?"

He gave a sincere explanation. He said that he had been promoted to the provincial capital less than three years ago. Before that he had lived in seclusion in countryside, an ancient and dilapidated small village. Like many other people, quite possibly he might have grown old and died in the same village. He believed that the secretary-general must know who had allowed him to leave and to attain the position he held today. He gave an example. If a person came into the world sucking his father's marrow and his mother's breast milk, could he possibly turn round and stamp on his parents?

The secretary-general told him that he was wrong. It was not a question of anyone trampling on anybody else, it was a question of making that person use medicine to cure his parents' sores, to remove the thorns from their flesh. He explained: he was unable to find any sores or thorns on his parents' bodies, because such dirty things had never existed there. The secretary-general said that he was wrong again and counselled him: the organisation is composed of countless elements. Was it possible that every Party member and cadre was free of defects? Pointing this out, he told him to think carefully, but just as before his words had no effect. The secretary-general sighed, and then warned: if you persist in dragging your feet, and others continue to view you as a backward element, it may

delay a promising political future ... This, he understood, was a reference to his appointment as head
of the vice-secretariat.

Afterwards he left the small red building and went
into the garden compound of the seat of the provincial
government. He walked along a flagstone path covered
by the red paper of spent firecrackers. A woman called
to him from the lush green grass in front of a round
platform. He knew her. She was the wife of the secretary-
general. He stopped.

This woman asked: "Wei, have you seen my old
man?"

"Uh-huh," he responded, "he's in the library
room."

This woman instructed him, "Go and get him for
me."

"O.K."

He turned and headed back towards the small red
building, mulling over her choice of words. She had
not used "please". He'd thought of her as an intellectual woman with a relatively high cultural level. As he
walked there unconsciously rose in his mind a feeling
of disgust. The wife of the secretary-general general-
ly did as she pleased, she ought to speak in a more
refined manner, she ought to act in a way more
appropriate to her and her husband's positions.

That evening, alone as usual in his three-room apartment, he smoked and drank tea, and then lay down
on his bed, trying to choose between "backward element" and "vice secretary-general". He remembered
the secretary-general's advice and his warning. From
the secretary-general himself his thoughts moved to his
wife, he remembered that she never said "please".

His thoughts swiftly cleared, he rolled over and stood up, and following his belated train of thought wrote a big-character poster.

The big-character poster was titled: "Please Do Not Allow Your Wife To Meddle In Politics". The rhetoric and tone of the words were extremely polite. He wrote that he was a good provincial head who enjoyed high prestige and commanded wide respect, and that his wife was also extremely kind and amiable. He tactfully criticized her, writing that on occasion his amiable and kindhearted wife said or did things that others might misunderstand. He hoped and was confident that in the future she would improve her behaviour. He omitted the numerous examples of her imperious attitude toward her husband's subordinates. This big-character poster was not up to anyone else's in the provincial government office, but in any case he had made some progress. His colleagues paid attention, there were fewer obstacles and there was already the possibility of a formal announcement of his promotion to head of the vice-secretariat.

The next day was extremely fine. The bright sun set off the azure blue sky, and on the horizon a wisp of cloud floated along with the wind. But for no apparent reason the world had descended into a heavy haze. As the movement spread like wildfire, more and more activists were labelled rightist. As the movement shifted direction the secretary-general continued to occupy his post as the head of the new leadership committee. And as before, his wife meddled in politics. Both the subordinate and his "Please Do Not Allow Your Wife To Meddle In Politics" poster were immediately referred to the committee for discussion. But the sheer number

of cases of former activists overwhelmed his own. And
for these other cases they had irrefutable evidence.
Three times they increased the quota of rightists
needing to be labelled, but he was never caught in the
net. It appeared that he was only small fry. For several
months he was on tenterhooks. The storm passed, and
with it his opportunity to be vice secretary-general.
Nevertheless, he had pulled through. The secretary-
general's wife said: "Boo, wait and see!"

The thirty-two-year-old man shuddered. The cigarette
burned his finger. It had smouldered almost to the butt
before he extinguished it. He took a sip of tea, rinsed
his mouth and spat the dark green tea back into the
gleaming white cup. Then he opened the door and
went into the room with the balcony. He opened the
door in that room and walked into the hallway where
he paced back and forth, his steps light and slow.
After a moment he stopped in front of the study. A
shaft of light streamed through a tiny crack. His body
pressed lightly against the door and it opened. The
light in the study was dazzling. Someone was sitting in
the revolving chair, and viewed from behind, resembled
him, although the back was quite clearly narrower and
lovelier than his. He knew that it was his cousin. She
was not yet in bed but was sitting dazed and bored in
the chair by the desk.

He walked in silently.

My uncle was the only intellectual in the family. He had
only received five years of home tutoring, but this had not
prevented him from becoming the most accomplished
intellectual in our town. Uncle was also a legend.
In 1952 he began to work as a neighbourhood secre-

tary in the township. He was in this extremely mundane position for one year. It was in the second year that he began his meteoric rise. He leapt over township, district, county, and regional levels, levels that most industrious people struggle their whole lives to attain, hardly expecting to get even halfway up. He cut across these vast strata and arrived in the provincial capital. There he became a secretary in the provincial government. After this he did not return to his hometown, but his influence was tremendous. Later, everyone who interviewed me wanted to know what the crucial factor was for my superior scholastic achievement and subsequent success. My answer was always exactly the same.

I said, "My uncle is a great intellectual."

The things my uncle left in his hometown included a sheet of paper from his schoolbook on which he had copied the Tang poet Li Mi's *The Plea to Your Majesty* in very small handwritten characters. His strokes were compact and neat, and his style forceful and confident. His greatest influence was on people's imagination. I had never cared about whether or not he became the vice-head of the provincial secretariat. He was undoubtedly a man of great learning. When he lifted his brush from the page, a string of beautiful pearls rolled out onto the paper. The power of his imagination was magical. To speak candidly, my father scorned studying, and on more than one occasion he advised me to leave school and learn a skill like mat-making, net-weaving, carpentry, or bamboo carving and go out and earn my living. For a time my family fell on difficult times and I had to earn money to supplement our income. I learned such crafts, attending two days of school and then working one. I relied on the extra money I earned for my tuition. In those days the end result of school was working in the fields, so why did I so stubbornly follow this absurd route? Because I wanted to be a great intellectual. My uncle was, I thought, so I should be one as well.

My uncle was not a rightist. I considered his political misfortunes to be the unavoidable lot of great intellectuals at that particular period. In 1957 his disaster was imminent, but he was not a rightist.

My uncle married twice. His first wife was an illiterate peasant woman whom he married before he became a neighbourhood secretary. Afterwards they divorced and she returned to her remote and desolate village, and in her ignorance tragically and plaintively passed the rest of her life. He met his second wife when, in his capacity as neighbourhood secretary, he attended an ordinary conference in another part of the country. She was exceedingly beautiful. He did not abandon her when he was promoted to the provincial capital, and they married at the beginning of the year in which he was nominated for provincial vice general-secretary. Half way through the year she became pregnant. But in the end she lost the child. Four years later she gave birth to a daughter as beautiful as she. That child was my cousin.

There is another reason why I worshipped my uncle. I envied the irrefutable rights he had over my cousin. In my childhood all of my exceptional efforts came from my sedulously imitating my uncle. I wanted to make myself become like him, to possess his erudite learning, and possess as he did my beautiful cousin.

A thirty-two-year-old man entered the study in the middle

of the night. That evening his cousin was sleeping in that room. After he walked into the study he stayed there.

The first time I saw my cousin she was eight years old. She stayed at my house for one month. Her family was again in desperate straits. On what they knew to be the eve of the impending disaster, her parents sent her home as a temporary avoidance measure. Perhaps she still did not understand what was going on. But there is one thing that is certain, she had no memory of her father's past glory. That year I was twelve, and in the first year of middle school. She returned over summer vacation. I was making mats every day decorated with beautiful designs. I had a quota of two per day, for which I was paid two yuan fifty, enough to buy twenty *jin* of cornmeal at the official price. I would fill my quota in half a day and spend the rest of my time studying.

I also found time each day to play with my cousin. I would take her on walks through the woods at the back of where we lived, teaching her how to recognise different kinds of trees and showing her the peach and pear trees that I had grafted all by myself. I would take her on walks along the river that flowed behind our house. The two of us cast a long and a short shadow across the limpid water. We walked along the broad riverbank. There was a kind of weed on the banks that looked just like spinach, except that it was huge, taller than a man. The locals called it "wild spinach" and we played hide-and-seek there.

There was an ancient, arched, stone bridge across the river. The stones were thin and narrow and it seemed rather insubstantial. Terror suddenly seized my cousin; she thought that the bridge would collapse as soon as anyone touched it. I walked nonchalantly onto the bridge. She hesitated for a moment and then followed. We crossed the bridge and climbed to the top of the embankment to watch the sun setting in the western sky. It was a rare sight that I never saw again: the scarlet sun as big as a bamboo basket. We pointed at it and my cousin said that it was as red as blood. I said no, it looked like a teardrop. She glanced at me in astonishment, and then looked back at the western sky. After a moment she turned her head and said: "Yes, it looks more like a teardrop."

During those years I studied desperately.

I would often fall into a daze. As the two of us walked along, I would suddenly go into trance, staring at a tree or a blade of grass, a river or an embankment, or some other bit of scenery. It seemed as if I were the only one left in the world, and I no longer felt frail. Only when my cousin shouted at me would I recover my senses. In a flash I realised what had happened: just then she and I had merged into one. How could that be? Was it because of our shared bloodline?

It was not the right season for grafting, but I still gave her a demonstration. I grafted a pear shoot onto another pear seedling. I also grafted a peach tree. My grafting knife was very sharp and my movements practised. I did it in the twinkling of an eye, but as I waved my hand my middle finger hit the knife, instantly sending out a stream of blood. My cousin immediately put my fingers in her mouth and sucked on them.

My cousin was very beautiful. To be more accurate, when she was eight she already possessed signs of beauty in her skin and outline. I had never seen my cousin before, so to say she was beautiful was a kind of fantasy. I once saw the film *Love of the Goddess*, and I remembered the lines from a song: "The birds on the trees form pairs" as the scene of a man and a woman together blurred. Afterwards as I walked to school I hummed that tune, but my cousin had replaced that woman, and she was without a doubt extremely beautiful. Unquestionably, that extremely beautiful cousin had originated in my imagination. When I saw my eight-year-old cousin, I thought she was identical to the one in my earlier fantasy.

My cousin urgently stuffed my fingers into her mouth. I stared at the anguish on her face. I watched her red lips sucking vigorously. My middle finger had a limp, numb feeling which spread throughout my body. Perhaps she was sucking my blood. My blood slowly boiled with excitement as something flowed through its vessels, rashly, tenaciously harassing my reason, awakening something long dormant in my life. I realised that my eight-year-old cousin was unconsciously revealing a kind of concupiscent excitement.

I was twelve that year. I was always reading, poring over every book I could find. The varying levels and miscellaneous subject matter were way beyond me. Most were inappropriate for a twelve-year-old child.

I bent over and kissed my cousin. I kissed her forehead, her eyes, her cheeks, my middle finger still in her mouth. Her tender red lips sucked and wriggled.

Then I withdrew my finger and kissed her lips.

In 1957, a thirty-two-year-old man was in disaster. He finally understood; the seed that he had so carelessly planted as a twelve-year-old child had suddenly sprouted after twenty years.

Twelve years passed, and a man lay curled up under the blazing sun. In front of him was a flock of white-winged, red-footed geese. The geese strolled leisurely under the azure sky and white clouds. There was a world of difference between the fates of the man and the geese. Every night the man was roped and kicked and beaten with clubs. During the day he tended the flock of geese. He always walked carefully behind the flock, his hand holding a long bamboo cane. But he would never hit them with the bamboo. At this time a goose and a human being were of more or less equal value, and if he lost one of the birds it would be the same as losing his own inconsequential life.

Twelve years earlier, as disaster approached a thirty-two year old man, he understood that it was the sprouting of a seed he had unconsciously planted twenty years before. But he only half understood; later, this seed was to bear even more evil fruit.

In the middle of that night twenty years later, I walked into the study. Under the dazzling light, those rows of books were even more of a feast for the eyes. I had read them all. I noticed the book that my cousin was reading. It was the thickest and biggest book in the bookcase. There was practically nothing it did not contain. On the page she was reading there was only one word which attracted attention: "law".

I continued to approach my cousin, knowing what I wanted to do. Then she turned around and looked at me.

I said, "You're ... still ... awake?"

She also said, "You're ... still ... awake?"

The two of us said the same thing simultaneously. Our voices were dry and strained, as if something was stuck in our throats. I stood beside her and looked at the word "law". I placed my right hand on her shoulder. She did not stir. My normally cautious nature left me wavering on the military demarcation line: a step forward was into the flames of battle, a step back was into calm and tranquillity. I hesitated on that line for a while. Then I stroked her shoulders, sending a shiver through her body. I caressed them again, and she began to tremble. She turned around, looked up in surprise, bewilderment in her eyes. I said, "Cousin, do you still remember? That year, when I was twelve..."

The twelve-year-old boy walked out of school. Black flagstones under his feet and an azure sky and white clouds above his head, joy lingered on in his heart. The old gentleman had just rewarded him with an inkstone and a long, pointed writing brush made of weasel hair. The old gentleman's prize for the other students? Twenty whacks each with his ruler. The boy suddenly felt something was wrong. And sure enough, his classmates were outflanking him, anger in their eyes. The youngster began to run, but there was someone blocking the intersection in front of him. He spun round and headed into a large compound.

The students grabbed hold of him in the compound. Just then, a man came out of the building. He was wearing a robe, dark glasses, and carried a cane. He shouted: "Where do you think you are, that you can yell and howl like this?" He pointed with his cane at the two wooden signboards on the wall. The students realised that they had run into the township offices of the Kuomintang. The man was the town magistrate. He asked why they were fighting, and he obviously did not believe that a twelve-year-old boy's superior grades could cause his classmates to attack him. He had him recite from the classics, and he chose a selection from Zhuang Zi's writing. The youngster had no choice, so he stood with his feet together and his hands straight downwards as if he were at school and recited: "In the far north there is a fish, and his name is *kun* ..." When he had finished reciting, the magistrate told the children to go inside.

Someone sat at the desk transcribing, and the magistrate asked him to leave. He told the youth: "Copy that from start to finish." The boy sat at the desk on which was a register of names. He lifted the pen and copied reverently and respectfully. The magistrate and the other youths stood to the side and silently watched him. In an hour he had finished. The magistrate picked up the register and examined it, and then he said: "It's true, the younger generation will surpass the older!" Then he said to himself: "I really should not have made him copy it for nothing — I'll break the rules and have him leave his name."

The magistrate removed his sunglasses and turned to the last page. On the bottom left of the register were the words "magistrate" and "secretary" with blank spaces below them. The magistrate asked for the pen and signed his own name. Then he pointed at the list the youth had copied and asked the urchins: "Could you write such good characters?" They shook their heads. He then asked them: "Do you still want to bully him?'' Again the brats shook their heads. He asked: "Should I encourage him?" The urchins all nodded their heads in agreement. The magistrate pointed to the blank space below the word "secretary" and said to the twelve-year-old boy: "Here, sign your name."

Ten years passed and the eight-year-old girl was eighteen. That year she graduated from high school. She was already a beautiful woman. Her beauty stemmed from the passionate imagination of another. Her regular features and beautiful body very easily created the illusion of beauty. But she had not yet really reached maturity. Her body was still quite frail, she did not yet have a full figure, her hair lacked lustre, and her eyes were not very bright. Her family was still in straitened circumstances, and her heart carried within it the weight and bitterness of life.

The eighteen-year-old girl's luck had not been so good. In the second year after the resumption of the college entrance examinations, she correctly answered all the questions on the front page of the maths section and handed in her paper. The other half of the questions were printed on the other side, but in her inexperience she had not seen them. The omitted questions were worth a lot and the section had a big influence on her overall score. As a result her grades were only good enough for vocational school. An agricultural machinery school from a medium-sized city sent her a notice of admission. Her heart was torn. She was happy, upset, and hesitant at the same time. She had to make a choice. However, at the time she did not understand that it was an extremely important decision, a choice that would most certainly influence the rest of her life. Her teachers thought she should turn down the vocational school and continue studying for two years. They were certain that she would pass the exams into a well-known university. However, it was not up to her her mother cried: "You know life is very difficult for our family. Your father's problems have not yet been resolved. Graduating from a vocational school is better than being a worker any time. Go to the school!"

The eighteen-year-old girl took her battered old case and set off on her journey. Only afterwards did this turn out to be a thoroughly absurd and thorny road. She arrived in the scenic city. Four rivers flowed through the town. There was a stony mountain which jutted up sharply from the otherwise flat surroundings. The stony mountain and the rivers formed four small parks. Standing high on the city side of the river was a pagoda that had been built in the Tang Dynasty. The city was as ancient and as famous as the pagoda. The first character of the province's name was taken from this ancient city. The vocational school was next to the largest park, at the foot of the high stony mountain. The campus was green and beautiful, and one could look up and casually take in the beauty of the mountain.

When the girl arrived at the school, the weather had been cloudy and drizzly for days on end. On the third day the rain stopped, but the sky was still grey and dark. She and her roommates went to their first class, mathematics, the subject which had once tripped her up. It was higher mathematics.

When she walked into that strange, damp

classroom, almost all her classmates had already arrived. The professor had arrived even earlier. She casually found a place to sit over by the window. The bell rang for class to begin. The professor, who had already been waiting for a while, straightened up and began to lecture. She looked up and saw a middle-aged man standing at the rostrum. He was slightly balding, and she guessed that he must be more than fifty years old.

This was the first time that she saw him. She did not know that he was the class adviser, she did not know his name, she did not know his age. She did not know anything about him.

The man looked much older than he actually was. At night he was struggled against, during the day he tended the flock. His blood and bones had been pressed almost dry. He was physically and mentally exhausted and had shrivelled to skin and bone. Everyone said that he would not live for more than a few days. However, he persevered. He lived through the overturning of heaven and earth, the "cultural revolution ". The benefits he received from the political changes were minuscule: his case was dealt with as an "contradiction among the people" but he was unable to recover his official status, his Party membership, or his original salary level. He continued to persist, all the way until his daughter graduated from high school and went to vocational school. From the year when everyone was certain that he would die, he had struggled along for more than ten years. It was 1979.

That man's luck had run out in 1957. He was not a

rightist. For this he still had to pay a price, and his political misfortune extended into the future.

In 1979 the rightist issue was resolved throughout the country. That year I was a secretary in an independent administrative work unit. I was assigned specifically to take charge of such work.

That year I decided to get involved in my uncle's political problems. It was no good, he was not a rightist, so he did not fall within the scope of this rectification.

Whether it was the moisture from the rivers, the call of the mountain, or the stimulating city life, the eighteen-year-old girl did indeed become beautiful. She changed with each passing day, her face growing fair and soft, her skin more elastic, her arms plump and white as lotus roots, and her legs full and round. Her eyes were bright, her eyebrows curled slightly upward, and her waist grew soft and curvaceous. When she walked her body swayed gracefully ... her face had more of a smile, and her heart brimmed with happiness. She herself was aware of all this. The eyes of the opposite sex, her mirror, the envy of her classmates told her.

The eighteen-year-old woman found more and more pleasure in washing herself. The school had a students' shower room, open every Tuesday, Thursday, and Saturday afternoons. It was free. Except during vacations, she never missed the chance to shower. But the shower hall was so small and there were so many students, each time she got under the shower head there were two or three students waiting around her. She was never able to really enjoy herself and would regretfully share her spot with someone else.

In what seemed a short time the school held mid-
term exams. It so happened that her calculus exam
was on a Saturday afternoon. She had done extremely
well in this class. She had arranged ahead with one of
her classmates to bring a change of clothes and their
shower things to the classroom. It took them just an
hour to finish the three-hour test. The two girls handed
in their papers, grabbed their clothes and shower
things, and charged off to the showers, laughing and
shouting all the way.

They arrived early. The shower room appeared silent, spacious and still. They quickly stripped off their
clothes and chose a spot. The girl turned on the shower, adjusted the temperature, and, without taking the
time to appreciate her beautiful figure, plunged her
naked body into the embrace of the gushing water. In
the twinkling of an eye, the soft, gentle, translucent,
warm water kissed her budding, vital body. She gradually became aware of a ˙hitherto unknown feeling of
lack of inhibition. Her body delighted in the caresses
and kisses of the endless stream of water. After about
half an hour she sensed something. Her classmate was
calling her.

Her classmate wanted the soap. She passed her the
plastic soapdish. Her classmate then turned around
and faced her.

"You are really beautiful," she said.

The girl laughed and turned the hot tap. The temperature rose, and her numbed skin was further stimulated
by the heat. She continued to feel uninhibited.

Laughing, her classmate looked at her, and then suddenly fondled, no, caressed her right breast. Her hand
slid across her chest, her rough fingers marking her

white, upturned breast and her cherry-red nipple. Her classmate said: "You are so beautiful you make people want to throttle you!"

She was taken by surprise and instinctively retreated a step. She could not get used to such joking. Her classmate laughed uproariously, a muffled sound that reverberated through the empty shower room. The girl sensed that her friend's words really did contain some elements of truth: both envy and jealous. The friend was from a remote village. Her father was a powerful cadre. His daughter had unfortunately been born with a harelip. Though the opening had been closed by meticulous surgery, but there still remained a long, thin scar which was enough to make this young woman in the flower of her youth unbearably ugly.

This ugly face and its previous actions produced a strong reaction in the eighteen-year-old. She momentarily felt a sense of revulsion, almost to the point of vomiting. Such emotions influenced her greatly, and she wanted to scream and rebuke her. Then, she remembered who her classmate was: she had come from the countryside as a Party member. She had unanimously been selected class monitor, was also secretary of their Communist Youth League branch.

It was certainly that feeling of political repression which had dogged her since birth and now filled the eighteen-year-old girl's veins that made her instinctively change her mind and suppress her anger. She smiled at her as before, the appropriate smile of someone who had been fooled. The two continued to shower.

Ten years passed and the girl was now twenty-eight. In that year her family split up. One day she went to her cousin's house. That night she stayed in his study. She did not feel like sleeping, so she picked up a thick book to read deep into the night ... deep into the night her cousin stole into the study. When she turned to look at him, she understood what he wanted. She saw the excitement and the desire in his eyes. She was uneasy about what she saw there. She did not say anything, instead kept it to herself. She did not resolutely resist, neither did she enthusiastically go along with it. She let everything seem natural. Her cousin bent down to kiss her, he kissed her forehead, her eyes, her cheeks ... then he also kissed her mouth. It was the same sequence as when he was twelve and she was eight. But she knew that she was no longer eight and he was no longer twelve. Twenty years had nourished one and ravaged the other.

That night they were together in the room.

Her cousin pressed against her, and she pushed him away. But she felt that she should not treat him like that. She did not understand why she had done so.

The light in the room was very soft.

Her cousin pressed against her again, and she did not push him away.

She did not think she was waiting.

Her hands and feet were cold, and her soles and palms were covered in sweat. She breathed deeply and looked at her cousin. Again she saw the excitement and desire in his eyes.

She was still uncertain. She really did not understand him. Did he love her? Pity her? Was it purely lust? Was it the stimulus of the same bloodline?

In the end she did not express her doubts, neither did she refuse him. She had trouble determining whether or not he was the same as the boy of twenty years before, but she knew that this year he was thirty-two years old. He was the same age as another man.

She felt that she did not have any rights. It was just like before, when she had no right to refuse another man. Today, she had no way to refuse her cousin, who was the same age as that man.

Ten years before, the girl had been in the grip of a deep political fear and was unable to fight with her class monitor and decisively sever relations. That ugly woman had played a cruel joke on her in the women's shower. The girl had committed a fatal mistake. It was her ugly class monitor who had made her accept him. She plunged into a terrifying trap, a trap that was not man-made, but the particular product of history and society. It was the Will of Heaven.

There was something else about my cousin that attracted people's attention: she had superior grades in all her classes. In her third semester at the school she was selected class representative for her calculus class. This important assignment brought her into direct contact with her class adviser.

The class adviser was as usual morose and depressed. The class' shock at learning his age was already well in the past. My cousin had heard about it in her dormitory. There were eight people in her room, including the ugly class monitor. The class monitor and the class adviser were from the same hometown, and the first time she mentioned his real age it surprised the other six classmates so much that for a long time they could not stop talking. My cousin blurted out: "You're saying that he is the same age as my cousin? How's that possible?''

Not only my cousin but all her classmates knew the full details about the class adviser. He was born into a poor peasant household. In the year when they were accepting the last intake of worker, soldier, and peasant students there was a place at the agricultural machinery school. None of the children of those in power were interested. The rule then was that if you came off the commune you had to return to it. After some calculations, he sold his family's only pig and used the money for presents and in the end obtained the place. And when that group of worker, soldier, and peasant students graduated he had some good fortune. He was allocated a job at the school. As one of the younger generation, he naturally took on the demanding task of class director.

The experiences of this contemporary of mine reflected his appearance: prosaic and unexceptional. As class representative requiring essential contact with him, my cousin turned a blind eye, just as she had no interest in her dormitory, her classroom, or her desk.

At the beginning of the third semester my cousin saw him at least twice a day: she handed him the class' homework, she picked up the corrected notebooks, and then she passed them back to everyone. For a long time they almost never talked. He was not yet entitled to a single room, so every morning he sat alone in his office. When my cousin went to collect the notebooks he would look at her silently. She would say: "Goodbye, teacher." His eyes would continue to follow her. After the last class of the afternoon he would return to the office to sit alone, and when my cousin handed in the homework it was a repeat performance of the morning.

This contemporary of mine was a man of few words. He was the same after he married my cousin. People always said that this reticence arose from a feeling of inferiority. My cousin said no, that was only half of it. The other half was that he was adept at scheming and plotting.

But that can be discussed later.

Before this my cousin had contact at least twice a day with her class adviser. She was not at all on her guard. She was unable to sense the enormous danger that was pressing ever closer and which suddenly seized the small town. One group fell into the net first. They were the small town's intellectuals. Twenty years before they had been a group of urchins tutored by the stately old gentleman. Between 1949 and 1957 they had found positions in the new government. Amongst their former classmates was one who was outstanding. At the beginning he had worked like everyone else in a very low position, but afterwards his career took off like a rocket and he transferred to the provincial government. Because of his exceptional talent, they suffered extra beatings at the hands of the old gentleman. Today they respected him; he had spared no effort to impart knowledge. They also took some pride in the bright future of their classmate.

When they encountered political misfortunes they were filled with ardour and sincerity. Wasn't it to remove thorns from and purify the skin of their parents? They searched carefully, not overlooking even the smallest suspicious blemish. But in the end they paid the price.

In fact there was at least one amongst them who

could have avoided the storm and escape unscathed. Though willing and enthusiastic he was incompetent. When they were at school, he was renowned as an idiot. Today he could not accept the label "backward element". That night, taking with him some Flying Horse cigarettes, he went to see one of his classmates. He implored him to allow him to sign his name at the bottom of a cartoon. Thinking of the cigarettes and their friendship, the classmate nodded his agreement.

The next day, the cartoon was pasted up on the wall. A silly little fish had used all its energy to swim into a net it could not see. That day was the day they hauled in the net.

Twenty years later that group of young ruffians became rightists and were sent off to a mountain on the border of the county to do hard labour. The mountainside was covered with waist-high scrub and a reddish-yellow earth that stretched for as far as the eye could see. The layer of soil was very thin, and just beneath it were dark brown rocks, a kind of precious brown iron ore with a very high iron content. To extract this they used iron hammers and steel drills to bore holes which they stuffed with dynamite. After explosions, rocks of all shapes and sizes covered the mountainside. They carried these rocks to a clearing at the base of the mountain, where there was a railway track winding towards a large city in the neighbouring province. After they had loaded the funnel-shaped cars, the whistle blew and the train headed off into the distance.

Later, jurisdiction over the mountain was transferred to the city in the neighbouring province.

They worked every day for eleven hours, from six in

the morning until six in the evening. At noon they had a half-hour break for lunch and then another thirty minutes to rest. The communal fare was very coarse. The portions were fixed: at breakfast two bowls of vegetable gruel, at lunch one bowl of bean cake and dry rice accompanied by one salted vegetable. They would suck on the bitter, salty vegetable, but quickly swallow down the bowl of bean cake and dry rice. After eating lunch they would lie down to sleep. Occasionally they would talk amongst themselves.

At first there was only shock. Their destiny was both horrible and absurd. Fate seemed to have taken the students, who had studied and learned at the hands of the old teacher and his ruler, and placed them on a narrow road from which there was almost no escape. Did their successful classmate far away in the provincial capital count? It seemed he had never felt the old man's ruler. His former classmates very much wanted to know what his fate was in that all-encompassing political storm.

News came that he had lost the position of vice-secretary-general when it was almost in his grasp, but otherwise he had escaped unscathed.

There was a small disturbance on the mountain, but it quickly subsided. The famished workers as usual received their bowls of bean cake and dry rice, but the vegetable portions were messed up. The stupid one, whose reactions were slow so that he was usually at the end of the queue, did not get any. He held his bowl in front of him, staring dejectedly. After a while each of his former classmates tore off a piece of their vegetable and threw it into his bowl. He began chewing, warm tears streaming from his eyes.

He said: "We've suffered enough, and there is no one who will save us!"

After eating, they sat close together. Everyone understood to whom he was referring. They huddled on the mountainside, the resplendent sun above them and luxuriant grass below. But the sun and the fragrant grass belonged to another world. They clasped their hands behind their heads as the image of a man high above them floated before their eyes. This man was strolling leisurely and insouciantly, unwilling to return to his home.

The idea arose spontaneously, it did not originate from anyone in particular. There was no first or last here. It passed simultaneously through the minds of those who had once been struck by that ruler. They all spoke out at the same time.

They wrote a letter and signed their names.

The beautiful student did not sever relations with her class monitor, neither did she intentionally try to distance herself from her. On the contrary, she tried hard to keep up their friendship. She did not hope to derive any benefit; her reaction was purely instinctive. As before she did not miss the chance to shower, and her class monitor always accompanied her. The class monitor had only joked once, that time in the shower. Afterwards the ugly woman shifted her attention and talked about their class adviser, about his poor family, his scheming when applying to school and upon graduation. She praised him again and again. My cousin could not understand why she was always talking about him.

The class monitor said: "I'm in love with him, I want to marry him. I want to have a date with him — will you come with me?"

My cousin was not surprised. The two of them seemed to be quite a good match: one old before his time, one deformed at birth.

She responded: "If it's a date, shouldn't just the two of you go?"

The class monitor answered: "He wouldn't dare. You know that teachers and students are not allowed to have romantic involvements."

The beautiful girl accompanied the ugly one on her date with her lover. The three of them did not attract any attention. They began to spend more and more time together. They strolled slowly along the bank of the Yangtze River, walked around the old brick pagoda, climbed the stony mountain, strolled through the thick forest, scooped up the clear river water in their hands ... occasionally he would shift his gaze to another target. The beautiful girl was completely unaware. Here were two worlds, the one of her class adviser and class monitor and the love they were weaving, and Nature. She belonged to the winding river, the rushing water, the lofty ancient tower, the green forest, the red flowers and the deep blue sky.

The beautiful girl passed messages between the two. When she went to pick up or drop off homework, she would discreetly pass him a small note with the class monitor's handwriting. telling him the time and the place.

That year she was nineteen. It was her second year at the agricultural machinery school and in three months she would graduate.

Only once did the class adviser set the time and the place for a date: dusk on Saturday behind the mountain, the place they had been on their very first date. As she handed in the homework he said that he had already told the class monitor and that there was no need to mention it to her. That day after class, the class monitor went off on some errand, so she went alone to the shower room, and when she returned to the dormitory there was still no sign of the class monitor. She looked at the time and guessed that she had gone on ahead. She combed her hair and headed towards the mountain.

As she walked up the mountain another person was heading down. It was a woman who had obviously been crying. Her eyes were red and swollen. They were on the same road, but they did not meet for as soon as she caught sight of the girl heading towards her, she immediately turned into the woods and followed another path.

The girl arrived at the rendezvous point, but there was no one there. She checked her watch. The three of them were always very punctual. She assumed that she must have made a mistake about the place. Just then the class adviser walked out from the woods behind her. At that moment the sun vanished behind the mountain.

At dusk that night, the rightists from the small town finished their letter. It was quite common in those days to write this sort of letter — "perform meritorious service to atone for one's crimes". They had two objectives: first, to be rewarded and have their "hats" removed; second, to let their classmate taste some of the bitterness they were experiencing in their lives.

The result was not what they had expected. As to the first objective, their "hats" remained in place until 1979. As to the second objective, the hardships their classmate suffered were even greater than their own and continued after 1979.

At dusk that evening, the beautiful student arrived as arranged behind the mountain. Her class adviser kept staring at her. His gaze was different from that of days past, probably because he had another objective in mind. She felt rather uncomfortable, but assumed she was mistaken. She waited patiently, but the other person still did not appear. It gradually grew darker. The rendezvous was in fact only meant for two people. She looked up at her class adviser, and suddenly saw the excitement and lust in his eyes. She knew what was wrong.

She said: "The class monitor still hasn't come? I'll go find her." The class adviser continued to stare at her. Wrinkled skin covered his bald head. He looked like an old man gazing at a small girl, a senile old man scrutinizing a beautiful doll. After a moment he said: "She's already been. She left, and I waited for you."

She understood. How was it possible? She asked, "Teacher, you know quite well that I have just been accompanying her ... she says that she loves you very much, that she wants to marry you!"

He said: "Apart from that, she doesn't want to return to her hometown. She wants to stay at the school after graduation. That's her biggest goal. What you mention are all smaller goals. For her, small goals are always subordinated to the larger one."

She was stunned.

He continued: "From the beginning of last semester I have met you twice a day. Strictly speaking, that was part of my work, and you and I did not really have any kind of interaction. Later, when she had the idea to bring you along ... that was when we really started to have contacts. That was her contribution."

She wanted to say: "I have never really had a conversation with you," but he waved his hand to stop her.

He said: "Just now she left in tears. She wasn't unhappy, she was excited — she seemed to be extremely satisfied. I agreed to allow her to remain at the school after she graduates."

He stopped, looked at her silently, and then said, in a deceptively casual tone: "In our class only two students are allowed to be employed by the school after graduation."

She understood.

In 1981 my uncle recovered his cadre status and took up an ordinary job. They still had a thick file on him. He was unable to recover his Party membership, his salary rank or responsibilities. My aunt sold off everything they had of value and went alone to the provincial capital to fight for his complete rehabilitation.

In 1981, just before her graduation, my cousin returned home to look for a job. She did all she could through the relevant channels at the county agricultural machinery bureau, but the results were all the same: she was sure to be sent to a village in the north-west part of the county, an extremely remote and desolate area. My cousin thought of it as a savage and cruel place.

During the "cultural revolution" my uncle had been appallingly mistreated there. My cousin swore that she would rather die than see that place again. What drove my cousin to tears was that my uncle was as powerless to help her in her job assignment as he was in dealing with his political problems. She could only resign herself to fate.

It was the class monitor who started spreading the rumours. She would say: "Haven't you heard? The mathematics class representative and the class adviser are having an affair." No-one believed her, so she would add: "Did you know that they have been secretly dating since last semester ... to avoid suspicion, they took me along as cover." Everyone thought she was letting her imagination run away with her. But she kept talking about it, regardless of the time, place, or person. Everyone grew sick of it. So they dragged this harelipped woman along to see the mathematics class representative to check her story. To everyone's surprise, the beautiful class representative neither rebuked her nor clarified the situation. She just murmured something, arousing everyone's suspicions.

Towards the end of the semester the class adviser spoke to the class. In just a month everyone would graduate, and now he was responsible for job distribution. Many of the students secretly coveted the jobs at the school. All kinds of intrigues slowly took shape. Good friends suddenly became enemies, rumours and gossip flew back and forth, and anonymous letters ap-

peared. No-one realised that their efforts were completely in vain. The class director had already gone into battle for his love.

As the last class ended and the students began to
leave, the class adviser remained after the lecture. Suddenly he called out loudly to his class representative as
she was about to leave:

"Let's go for a walk!"

Everyone stopped in their tracks and looked round.
As they watched in astonishment, the beautiful class
representative walked out with her withered teacher.
She had a hesitant expression on her face, and her
body seemed to follow him against her will. But he
was not holding a knife and forcing her to go. In the
end she left with him.

The students were enraged. This was not just a bolt
from the blue; it was undoubtedly a public challenge.
This was still 1981, and young people were not yet lib-
erated in their attitudes. They were unable to follow up
their thoughts or ideas with action. They could only
swallow their anger and act as if nothing had happened.

The two did not return to their former points of
assignation. There was no longer any need to go to
the river's edge, the pagoda, or the forest. There was
no longer any taboo; they no longer fell into that category that prohibited teacher-student affairs. Everyone
knew that in less than a month she would start her
new job.

The class director took his beautiful student and in
broad daylight paraded brazenly around the campus
with her. He wanted to announce to everyone that
what had once been seen as sheer nonsense was

actually indisputable fact. As they walked, the picture of the two lovers, one ugly, the other beautiful, caused a tremendous sensation and left a deep and indelible impression on the minds of everyone at the school.

The net was pulled tighter and tighter.

There was still no way to describe the making of the trap. Was it man-made? Or was it the special product of history and society? Was it the will of Heaven? That it was incredibly strong was certain, and once formed it was ubiquitous. It disdained history and society and despised time and space.

In 1957 there was a woman who was criticised for meddling in her husband's political affairs. Her scheme to seize the opportunity and bring about revenge failed, and she angrily declared: "Hai, wait and see!"

There was a mishap: a student became pregnant. It was her ever-expanding belly that gave her away. She had tried to strap a leather belt around her stomach to stop it from growing, but that did not work. The person who got her into trouble was her class monitor. He had only been at school for a year. He was dismissed from his post as class monitor and kicked out of the Communist Youth League. He was interrogated before he was disciplined. His interrogators were very patient, and he told them every detail. He explained that altogether he had had sex with her twice. The first time was not very successful; the second time he had succeeded, but the consequences had been disastrous.

At dusk one evening, the beautiful student accompanied her class adviser into his office. The class adviser had still not been given a single room. They were alone. He told her about the unlucky student and his girlfriend. He meticulously described the interrogators' questioning and the troublemaker's confession. It was as if he were standing at the lectern, casually and absorbingly analysing an extremely subtle mathematics problem ... darkness had fallen long ago. They had not turned on the lights.

In the blackness he suddenly stopped speaking. There was a sudden intake of breath, and then he reached for her.

The beautiful girl's only response was to think of the words "job distribution". She tried hard to clear them from her mind and concentrate on dealing with reality. In fact this was the first time that he had ever really touched her. She was startled to discover that his method was even more direct than in books or films or her own imagination.

She started to think about all the bad things about him: his uneducated peasant family, his age ... his barbaric excitement and lust, his savage possession of her ... but she wanted to think of other things. Her thoughts became unclear, and she allowed him to do as he pleased.

That night, he had sex with her as that unlucky student had had sex with his girlfriend.

In 1981 in a scenic city, at a vocational school, a woman tasted forbidden fruit for the first time. This girl did not wait until they were officially married before she began to obey her future husband. For a woman of her times, of that society, and of that race, she had undoubtedly committed an error. In the days to come she would pay the price.

This was only the first mistake. There was also a second and a third.

The two of them dressed and he turned on the light. A smile on his old face, he said: "Now, you won't stay on at the school and dump me, will you?"

The beautiful girl made her second mistake. She said: "You have already done this to me ... how could I dump you?"

He laughed. It was a wanton, shameless laugh that revealed all his wrinkles. His laugh enveloped her, and in her daze she thought of a picture she had seen when she was a child: a cat had caught a mouse, bitten off its feet, and let it squeak and toss about helplessly on the floor as it walked around it ...

And then she went on to make her third mistake. She said: "You won't dump me and not let me stay at the school, will you?"

He was startled, and his smile momentarily disappeared.

It was too late for her to retract her words. His withered face took on an expression she had never seen before of solemnity and conceit.

In the end my aunt went to see the man who had been provincial secretary-general in 1957. She went to his home. He was still the secretary-general. He had fallen during the "cultural revolution" and suffered tremendous hardship. But he had pulled himself back up, returning to his original job and his original apartment. What made him feel extremely guilty was the fact that he had brought disaster on his wife as well. However, other people had a different opinion. They said that the mental and physical torment that he suffered was in large part caused by the grievances people had against his wife.

My aunt first met the secretary-general's wife. She did not come straight to the point. She had given them five hens, fifty *jin* of shelled peanuts, and five *jin* of ground sesame oil. These were her last and only magic weapons. She had offered everything that she had. She understood that the people in this house held her husband's fate in their hands.

She wanted to ask him to countermand the order he had issued twenty-four years before under his wife's influence.

My aunt was about to raise the issue when she suddenly changed her mind. She did not reveal her identity. She only asked the secretary-general to personally concern himself with the case of her innocent husband. She followed her intuition. Her intuition was correct. The secretary-general's wife's memory had been damaged by the disasters through which she had accompanied her husband, and everything that had happened twenty-four years before had become a blurred dream.

His wife still meddled in his political affairs. She asked her husband, "Aren't you always complaining? How many years of hardship did you endure? This man has suffered for twenty-four years! Isn't that enough? Isn't about time to completely rehabilitate him?"

My aunt omitted anything that might jog the memory of the secretary-general's wife. She only told her the general story. The wife did not feel like reading the appeal letter. She only knew that twenty-four years before someone had been treated unjustly and that his case had still not been re-examined.

The wife said: "Here, approve this for him."

The secretary-general picked up his pen and wrote on the appeal letter: "Please assign someone immediately to re-examine and completely rehabilitate."

He signed his name. He had hardly read what was on the paper.

The secretary-general felt exhausted. The tempest had carried away most of his subordinates, and ironically he had been the driving force behind that storm. He often asked himself: Isn't this excessively cruel? No, it was not his fault. He had to obey orders from above, otherwise he too would be carried away by the turmoil. Eventually the storm subsided. He needed rest.

But that was not the end. That piece of paper brought trouble in its wake. It implicated someone here. It was a subordinate who had the good fortune to escape the terrifying storm. He was extremely talented but did not understand the ways of the world. At the start of the movement he kept his mouth shut, which caused others to reproach him, delaying his promotion to head of the vice-secretariat. He had personally tried to urge his subordinate to get on top of the situation. Eventually he acted, writing a big-character poster entitled "Please Do Not Allow Your Wife To Meddle In Politics". He clearly lacked common sense and was unfamiliar with the inner workings of families of high officials. It really was hard to admit that he, an illustrious and powerful provincial official, always accepted defeat at the hands of his nagging wife. That simple-minded genius had brought trouble on himself and on his superior — but fortunately those times had already passed.

The secretary-general smoked a cigarette as he considered the affair. It was a very clumsy letter. It reflected their desperation and fear as they tried to extricate themselves from political misfortune, and revealed, too, how despicable and unscrupulous they were as they tried to drag another down with them. There were two glaring errors that ran counter to common sense: a twelve-year old was only a child and incapable of counter-revolutionary activities; there was no way one could compare a KMT secretary to a Communist Party secretary. The former was just a common scribe, while the latter was a powerful leader of the first rank. The secretary-general shook his head and sniggered.

He put the letter back into its envelope and tossed it to one side. He had decided to ignore it.

In 1979 I was assigned to handle the rectification of rightists. I found the files of my uncle's classmates from twenty-two years before and put them where no one could find them. There were so many other files that they quickly disappeared in the shuffle. This group missed their first chance for rectification. They were all extremely anxious and one after another came to urge me but each time I dodged them. Rectification work had stalled, and when I met with them I told them what they wanted to hear so as to get them to leave. Not long afterwards, the order came down to deal with their cases, so I pulled out their files and announced that I would take responsibility for their re-examination and rectification. I did not hesitate to condescend to this job and went and talked to each one in turn. I was enthusiastic, meticulous, and extremely responsible. I searched everywhere for documents beneficial to their cases. Of course, I tried to make it very clear to them that I was exerting much effort on their behalf so as to make them firmly remember my name. More important still was to lead them to the following conclusion: without my hard work, their rectification would have remained in the distant future.

It was no doubt a clever way of exacting revenge on these men. Strictly speaking, it arose from base instincts. In fact I had a deeper motive: I was setting the stage for my uncle's rehabilitation. I wanted them to personally draw back their daggers.

When the secretary-general's wife strode into his office she was still choked with anger. They had argued over a big-character poster, "Please Do Not Allow Your Wife To Meddle In Politics", written by an insignificant little secretary who had dared to meddle in their private affairs. This young man should have been punished, but her husband had let him escape, explaining: there are too many people with serious problems, and this subordinate was insignificant and powerless. Although she knew that what he said made sense and her anger had subsided, she did not show that she had calmed down. A temporary cease-fire continued for a while.

At first she did not feel like looking at the letter casually tossed onto the desk, but then she noticed a sparkle in his eye. Slowly she traced its origin. She felt bewildered. Which bitch had written him a love letter? She snatched up the envelope and pulled out the letter. Then she grinned broadly.

She asked: "What are you going to do about this?"

The secretary-general said, "It's complete nonsense. Of course I am just going to ignore it."

She took no notice and slowly and carefully reread the letter. Then she began to read it aloud.

She omitted the line "Provincial government anti-rightist group" and read: "We anti-Party, anti-socialist, anti-people rightists who have committed serious crimes admit our faults and wish to reveal to this organisation a Kuomintang spy hidden in the provincial secretariat."

She ordered her husband: "Listen!"

She continued reading: "In 1937, when he was twelve years old, he entered the spy ring at the introduction of the ringleader of the municipal Kuomintang branch who was also serving as town magistrate. He added his name to the name list of this spy organization, and furthermore was appointed to the important post of secretary to the said spy organisation."

She read on: "The evidence for this incident is irrefutable and brooks no denial. When he became a spy and signed his name to the register, we were all standing by and witnessed it with our own eyes. On the last page of the register he wrote and signed his name under the title of secretary. The register is now in the archives of our county Public Security Bureau. If you send someone or make a written request, as soon as you see it you will understand."

At the bottom they wrote, "Our goal in doing this is to ferret out the bad person now concealed in the provincial secretariat and to purify that organization. At the same time, we wish to perform meritorious service to atone for our crimes. We have gradually come to understand the seriousness of our crimes and are determined once again to be good citizens. We hope the organisation will deal with us leniently and give us another chance.''

At the bottom of the page were their signatures. She read each one aloud in a sonorous voice.

She looked at her husband for a moment, and then began to speak. She spoke slowly and carefully. "You still want to protect him, don't you? Do you understand the seriousness of the situation? These rightists are just crazy. They won't wait long for news. They'll just concoct another letter and send it on to an even higher organisation. Are you really willing to pointlessly and criminally harbour him and then go down with him too?''

The secretary-general lit a cigarette. His wife crushed it out, grabbed a pen, and placed it in his hand.

"Write your instructions here,'' she ordered.

The secretary-general hesitated slightly, then lifted the pen and wrote, "This case is shocking and provides much food for thought. Please assign someone to investigate and deal with it seriously.'' He signed his name and the date.

In 1957, on an iron-rich mountain, a group of rightists wrote a letter. That letter had two objectives: to extricate them from their present troubles; and to bring about the downfall of someone who was always lucky. The final outcome was entirely different from what they had hoped.

In 1981, my cousin formally married her class adviser.

Because of their straitened economic circumstances, they held the wedding at the school. No relatives from either family attended. She was now working as a draftsman at a factory affiliated to the school. All her co-workers sent their congratulations. The guests had mixed feelings about the wedding. They sighed at the sight of the "fresh flower stuck in cow dung," and some sympathized with her. In order to remain at the school, and because she hated the idea of leaving the city, she had, for no better reason, ruined her beauty. The women quietly discussed the bride's wedding dress. It was a faint, almost completely faded red. It did not resemble a traditional wedding gown but made her look even more beautiful and charming. Some thought that she had purposely worn the dress in order to create such a dazzling contrast.

They were wrong. This was a one-of-a-kind dress which a seamstress had made for my cousin a week before. A wedding gown had to be red, so my cousin went to all of the fabric stores in the city and chose a very modest light red. The colour had been much brighter. She tried it on once in front of the groom then carefully put it away. Three days before the wedding, the groom mixed together some detergents, added a few chemicals, and used this concoction to wash the dress. On the day of the wedding, the bride went to open the kitchen cabinet, only to discover that her dress looked like a faded old flower. She burst into tears, but concealed them from her husband. The deafening sounds of exploding fireworks came from the campus. She wiped away her tears, put on the faded wedding gown, smiled wanly into the mirror, and then slowly walked out into the cheerful, happy atmosphere.

A woman with a hole in her lip was also among the crowd of well-wishers. She had plenty of reasons to congratulate them: the harelipped woman was her class monitor and classmate, and she was his student and neighbour at home. The woman with the hole in her lip tirelessly, happily ran around. Even the bride and groom grew tired, but she remained as excited as ever. On the second day, she reported to her former teacher what the women thought of the bride's wedding dress. This led to an even more tragic fate for the pathetic, faded garment.

At noon that day, the groom told the bride that there was a spot on her dress. He helped her to take the dress off, wash it, and hang it on the clothesline by their door. At dusk the woman went to bring in her precious dress, but the line was empty.

Accidentally she discovered the fate of her dress. When she went to the storehouse to get some tools, she passed a rubbish truck some way from her house. That was when she discovered it. What attracted her attention was the familiar, faded fabric. It had been heartlessly dismembered, unquestionably shredded by a pair of scissors.

She let out a long sigh and walked on past. When she returned home she did not mention the incident. She kept it stored away in her heart.

The harelipped woman, the former class monitor, also stayed at school after graduation. Every day she kept watch in the information office. She also distributed the newspapers and mail. Soon after the marriage of her beautiful classmate and her class adviser, she married a worker from the school. He was a weak and shrivelled little man.

The newly-weds were given a room in a low house in front of which was a row of even lower shacks. Every household used its space in the same way: the room in the house was the bedroom, the room in the shed was the kitchen.

As luck would have it, the beautiful bride and the harelipped class monitor were next-door neighbours. Only one wall separated their bedrooms and their kitchens.

The bride soon faded into insignificance. People began to look at her as a flash in the pan. She had been so fresh and sparkling. In an instant she had withered. It was a fatal, inexorable transformation. There was a not so bright period for this: after she had been together with her husband for two years she gave birth to his son. But this was not the reason. Even though she was born under an unlucky star, her decline should not have been so sudden. A form could often be seen hurriedly walking through the campus. Only a vague and hazy outline of her former beauty remained. People tried in vain to look back before those 720 days of wind, rain, clouds, and sun to find the beauty of her past, but they were left sighing even more deeply.

In the middle of the night when I was in my thirty-second year, I entered my study. That night my friendless, wretched cousin was staying there ... under the soft light, there remained an unreal, illusory outline of her former beauty. I saw only a withered, wan, and sallow figure.

After six months of marriage he finally bought his wife
a dress. At least he was satisfied with it. He searched
endlessly until he had made today's beautiful choice.
His wife tried it on and went over to the mirror. She
was so startled she let out a cry. For the first time in
her life she discovered that the style and colour of
clothes could distort and destroy her looks. She imagined how she looked: a shrunked, ancient Buddhist
nun, an old, ailing, trembling, shivering woman. She
took off the dress and threw it in his face.

His method of resistance was exceptional. He neither
spoke nor ate nor slept nor smoked for three days and
three nights.

He always smoked as if his life depended on it, but
now he suddenly stopped. That was what amazed her
the most. She put on the dress and went outside.

From then on people on the campus no longer saw
a beautiful girl. They only saw a dress of eccentric style
and colour walking back and forth under the blue sky
and bright sun.

Once the yoke goes round the neck, it draws tighter
and tighter ... unless you struggle with all your might
to free yourself.

In 1957 my uncle ran out of luck. He was not a
rightist. He was officially labelled "an historical counter-
revolutionary", a label that did not really fit him. The
disciplinary report stated: "In light of the fact that at
the time he was only twelve years old, he was clearly
immature   and   ignorant,   so   his   case   will   be

handled as a contradiction among people." He was removed from his post in the secretariat, kicked out of the Party, and his salary rank was lowered from grade 14 to grade 17. He was sent to a state farm to do hard labour. The farm was on an endless stretch of salty earth in the northwest corner of the province.

He retained his cadre status and received a monthly salary, but otherwise was the same as the other farm workers, doing daily manual labour. In politics he was not as good as they were. He was not allowed to read government documents, attend meetings, and if he had any outside business he had to formally ask permission to leave.

My aunt harboured some regrets after her marriage. Of course, she had not been in the least responsible for my uncle casting aside his first wife. He had met my aunt at a meeting while he was a neighbourhood committee secretary. Later, they fell in love. The two officially married, but only after my uncle had been promoted to the provincial secretariat. People ignored the preceding facts and just fixed their attention on their marriage. Rumours spread that the beautiful woman had married him for his higher social standing! My aunt was very hurt. Being misunderstood is not something that makes people happy. My aunt always wanted to prove that even if my uncle had remained a neighbourhood secretary for the rest of his life she would have loved him, married him, taken care of him, grown old with him... In 1957, my uncle's luck ran out, and my aunt's opportunity to prove herself had arrived.

It was certainly not what she had hoped for. It was imposed by external forces. It was an inescapable, cruel reality. But if she had really wanted to prove her words, then it was a gift from heaven.

That year she had a miscarriage. Only three years later did she give birth to her daughter. It was a tense time for her. Her work unit was constantly urging her to divorce her "historic counter-revolutionary" husband. She refused, and afterwards she too entered that barren land. She accompanied her husband through his troubles.

In the middle of that night, in that study, on that bed, two people held each other tightly, but for a long time they did not do anything. There was only a shrivelled person talking endlessly, incessantly...

This was what my cousin told me. In 1969 my uncle was sent to a place where he was both unable to live and unable to die. At night there was the insanity of mankind, and during the day there was the beautiful flock of geese. Everyone said that my uncle would not survive for very long ... afterwards, people said that if it had not been for his wife, he would have died many deaths.

In those days life was extremely difficult for him. Even under the big, white clouds he was unable to escape a feeling of suffocation. The strolling geese, the blue sky and white clouds above, the sun, the withered grass, the alkaline soil, they all reached out innumerable hands to strangle him.

My aunt would make one kind of food which she would take secretly to him as he tended his flock, in an attempt to nourish his withered body. The ingredients were simple. She would cut pork fat into strips, add sugar, and steam it. In normal circumstances it would be a disgusting mixture. But it was this mixture that rekindled his almost extinguished flame of life.

In 1969, my aunt would go each day to a small town four kilometres away. The town was not part of the state farm and no one recognized her. She would first go to the hospital and implore someone to take her blood. She sold the blood and used the cash to buy fresh pork fat and sugar.

In the long years after 1957, a rumour in my hometown died out. The original rumour was: "That beautiful woman is marrying him for his position." The rumour was forgotten, and people even forgot the two people whom the rumour was about.

Only by accident and on particular occasions would people mention the two, saying: "If it had not been for her, he would have already been finished!"

The eight-year-old girl spent her summer vacation at her cousin's house. When she returned home she saw a horrible scene. The disaster hanging over her family shocked her intensely. Slowly she adapted and became numb to it, as her mother had done.

Her mother grew weaker and weaker, and her skin began to look like yellowed wax paper. Every day she would force herself to go to the town to sell her blood, buy sugar and pork fat, and cook them. Her energy was just about exhausted. She had her eight-year-old daughter deliver the life-saving sustenance to her father where he was tending his flock.

She poured the boiling liquid into an enamel cup.

That way, even after carrying it for a kilometre and a half it would still be warm. The little girl wrapped a handkerchief around the steaming cup and carried it out through the door and towards the unploughed, hardened plain. She walked alone, following criss-crossing footpaths between the fields. She walked left and right, completing two large arcs, and then passed around a pond. She looked at a south-facing slope covered in wild grass almost two feet tall. She hastened her steps and climbed the slope. She saw the flock of snow white geese, and under the dazzling sun she saw a trembling old man.

Large though the state farm was, it was a sub-department work unit. The farm workers had long before shifted their attention from trying to leave the land to dealing with certain people. Large and small "wage revolution" committees merged into two large, evenly matched opponents. Unable to break with precedent, they used all the usual methods to show their revolu-tionary zeal: they tortured the man who had held power in the work unit. He was only a grade nineteen cadre, so simple-minded that often it was pathetic. The two factions dragged him onto the stage and slowly struggled against him until even they found it boring. Then someone discovered that on the farm was an inconspicuous larger target, a grade seventeen cadre, two grades higher than the farm chief! And previously his grade had been even higher, grade fourteen. He had been a secretary in the provincial government, and he had almost become head of the vice-secretariat. And of course, even before all of this, in 1937, he had been a secretary in a Kuomintang spy organization.

At four in the morning, a line of torches came screaming along, pulled him from his warm quilt, stood him up like a newly planted shooting range target, and dragged him off. As the first rays of dawn appeared in the eastern sky, most of the farm workers, at the command of the ear-splitting loudspeakers, rushed to the meeting ground. Everything was arranged and they were instructed to bring him on stage. Just then, the red sun slowly rose.

The grade seventeen cadre went on stage in the "aeroplane position". The props were very simple: two people, two sticks. This was a common position during that period: he was forced forward by the two people and the two clubs, his face towards the ground, his back towards the sky. The two ordered him to move. His movements were really like that of an aeroplane taking off. At first he walked firmly, neither slow nor quick, gradually their pace quickened and his steps became shuffles. Suddenly they were too strong for him and they shot forward violently, sprinting ahead, two people and two sticks framing a hunched-over body. The meeting ground was in the compound of the farm headquarters, and within the compound were two concrete roads. The two people leaped onto the stage. But the hunched-over body tripped up on the road, and the ground scraped off a large patch of skin from his forehead. The two lifted him up, and the hunched-over body staggered up onto the stage.

The farm workers recognised him. Normally he would quietly go about his work. They said that he was a grade seventeen cadre, that before that he had been a grade fourteen secretary in the provincial government, that he had almost been head of the vice-secretariat, that forty-two years before he had been a Kuomintang special agent ... how was it possible? But irrefutably he had been. That proved how cunning his camouflage was and how deep his cover. Thereupon arms were raised, slogans poured forth, and his crimes both past and present were enumerated. And then they spontaneously hit and kicked him.

The bent body remained hunched, and only his forehead looked alive as drops of fresh red blood fell to the ground. At the end of the meeting, there was a bowl-sized pile of wet, purplish-black soil.

But still it was not over. The other faction did not want to be left behind. Thereupon they started over from the beginning...

Afterwards, "revolution" switched to the evenings as during the day everyone worked to increase production. The hunched-over body's method of production was to look skyward while pretending to shake his bamboo cane as he struggled to keep up with his flock of chanting white geese.

Day after day the eight-year-old girl carried the enamel cup out of her house. She walked across the criss-crossing paths through the fields, saw a flock of snow white geese, and saw a man on the brink of collapse.

The child grew confused. Wherever she went there was greyish alkali floating in the air. She could not understand why she alone carried this scalding enamel cup, why she always walked along high and low paths, why she always headed towards a flock of snow white geese... Then she would mechanically pass him the cup. She did not recognize the person tending the geese. She wondered: Who is this man?

She knew that she and this man tending the geese had some kind of relationship, a relationship that could not be severed. Gradually, the cup she held in her hands, the criss-crossing paths between the fields, the swaying geese ... these images all began to fade, and in the end they disappeared. When she went out through the door, she leapt over everything else and saw only that sick, weak man.

The eight-year-old child carefully examined this relationship. She became clear that there was a force connecting them. It was a river. She clearly perceived the colour of the river and understood its essence. It descended from the heavens, stretching forward from antiquity, and flowed into his veins, flowed out again, and then entered hers. It was a river of consanguinity.

My cousin said that in 1969 her mother secretly and repeatedly sold her blood, to the point where she had almost sold her life to the hospital in the small town. People no longer saw a graceful woman; they only saw the dried-out shape of a body.

In a daze, the eight-year-old child was struck by an idea: she must make something for that stranger who tended his flock of geese.

In an instant she had aged, no, she had grown stronger. She seemed to have passed twenty years, to become twenty-eight, a mature woman, a woman capable of raising a son.

In her imagination she had turned into a mature woman. She wanted to give, to bestow upon him warmth and kindness. She really wanted to hold that man in her wide breast and to use her milk of life to moisten his withered body.

She did not succeed. In reality, there was no way for her to do that. Suddenly, she once again saw that river. She looked at its colour, its essence, and she saw that it was still a river of consanguinity. The river had changed its direction, and it now flowed between them. The river was wide and the waters were turbulent, coldly blocking the path between them.

But the idea remained, kept in the endless space of her life, reappearing time and time again.

The light in that study stayed soft.

The face of that withered person was red...

Puzzled, she said: "So that's the way it's supposed to be?"

Only after they married did the new bride really appreciate her husband's decrepitude. His baldness, the lines on his forehead, the wrinkles around his eyes, his stooped posture... These were the outward signs that he had, for no reason, aged an extra twenty years. What was even more frightening was his life-force. Once, she had mistakenly thought that his shredding of her wedding dress and his gift of that eccentric dress intended to ruin her beauty were an expression of his life-force. She was wrong. It was a kind of struggle. Except for when he lectured in class, he was reticent and his eyes were dull and lifeless. Occasionally he would hold a conversation, but he spoke delicately and weakly. His words seemed to be squeezed out in desperation from between two pallid lips; each word was exhausted.

She did not know there was such a thing as happiness.

From the day of their wedding, the bride and her husband walked shoulder to shoulder towards the end of their lives. Their speeds were different: he had an almost uniform pace, while she was definitely increasing in speed. Eventually she pulled ahead.

At a vocational school in that picturesque city, a class monitor got one of his female classmates pregnant. After that incident, a class adviser led a beautiful student of his into an empty and quiet classroom. Using the darkness as cover and the story of the other couple's misfortune as foreplay, he had sex with his beautiful student. He was not very successful, but he already had her wrapped around his finger.

The next evening he repeated his attempt. This time he succeeded.

After the class adviser and his student married, they both lost their original identities. Now one was a husband, the other a wife. The husband and wife always argued. Their quibbling was mostly a kind of shirking of responsibility. In the end, the husband used his stubbornness to wear her down and emerge victorious. He kept looking back and savouring the first two times he had done her. That was in the empty, quiet office, before they were married. The first time was not very successful, but he had already seized possession of her. The second time was extremely successful. He cherished the past and scorned the present. He was always complaining that it was her seemingly beautiful body that diminished his interest in her; she was always wearing a long face, making him unable to arouse any passion... He said that after she had borne the child he felt she was no longer the same. In his eyes, she was the same as an old woman.

He often said: "If I had known all along that it would be like this, I might as well have married her!"

"Her" referred to the next-door neighbour, the woman with the scar on her lip. Her classmate, his fellow villager.

His wife could no longer stand it. She could not measure the depth or the breadth of that bitter sea. Perhaps it had no bottom. She did not know how many more evil methods he would use to torture her. She considered whether or not to divorce him.

Secretly she returned home to her parents' house.

In 1984 my uncle was completely rehabilitated. It was entirely because of the power of the provincial secretary-general. He acted only after his wife had intervened. After the secretary-general had taken a clear-cut stand and issued the order for rehabilitation, my uncle recovered his grade seventeen cadre status that he had had when he worked on the state farm. Three years later he recovered his Party membership and his grade fourteen rank — the rank he had had originally when he was a secretary in the provincial government. That year he was assigned a corresponding position. Due to his health and advanced age, he worked as an adviser to the state farm.

In 1984 my cousin secretly boarded a long-distance bus. Three hours later she arrived in another city. Here she boarded a train to return to her parents' home. There were no seats, so when she stepped off the train her humiliated body was on the verge of collapse. All she wished was to throw herself into her mother's arms and have a good cry, purging herself of her bitterness and sorrow. She headed straight for her home, but as luck would have it there was a lock on the door. She went to the office to find my uncle.

My uncle had his own office. When my cousin walked in he was sitting in a yellow rattan chair behind the big writing desk. My cousin could not stop herself from opening her mouth and telling him everything. He listened to her patiently and silently. She only told him the general situation and her present thoughts. After all, he was her father and she was his daughter, and there were many details which she was unable to tell him. She finished. My uncle sat silently in his yellow rattan chair for a long time.

He said: "He seems rather old, but age has its advantages ... initially we didn't know ... you found him on your own."

He threw out a question: "What about your child? After all he is your own flesh and blood. Could you bear to see him have a stepfather or stepmother?"

My cousin was dejected. For a time she did not respond.

Shifting in his yellow rattan chair my uncle said: "What is the parents' greatest hope when their daughter grows up and marries? In most circumstances, they hope that the daughter and son-in-law grow old together. Of course they don't wish for the household to break up and for another son-in-law to appear ..."

My cousin's whole body went cold.

After my uncle's rehabilitation, his Party membership and 1957 cadre ranking were restored and he was assigned his own office and a position equal in rank to that of the head of the state farm. He had come full circle through his difficult experiences, returning to his position of twenty-seven years before.

His wife returned home but she did not explode at him. Her scheming husband felt something was wrong. He became very cautious and spied on her from dark corners. He waited tensely, but after a full two months nothing happened. In the end he could not contain himself. He removed his mask and returned to his old ways.

When rejected, he angrily, weakly berated her. When his desire swelled to breaking point but could not be satisfied, he screamed out the name of the ugly woman next door. But she did not erupt; she endured it all.

She worried that he was yelling too loudly, that the woman next door would hear him. From then on, for some reason she felt as if she had done something wrong to her neighbour. Even if she ran into her in the street she did not dare look at her in the eye. The woman sensed it clearly, but she could never guess the reason. The ugly woman would sometimes smile in her confusion, making the wife tremble with anxiety and fear, thinking that what appeared on that face was a smile omniscient and evil.

The days and months passed quickly. Life was bitter and tormented. She could see no end.

Every day the twelve-year-old youngster found time to play with his eight-year-old cousin. Happiness arrived with the summer vacation. They were reluctant to part, and their separation lasted too long, splitting the wondrous days of their youth. The second time they met was in that picturesque city. The two were so shocked they hardly recognized each other.

The youngster gave his cousin a tree-grafting demonstration. His grafting knife was sharp and his movements were skilled and dexterous. When he finished, he was a bit too complacent and as a result, his finger accidentally hit the blade, sending forth a stream of blood. His cousin grabbed his finger and put it in her mouth, sucking his wound between her wriggling, tender red lips. His warm blood flowed directly into her body. They originally shared the same bloodline. The youth had an odd feeling. He lowered his face and kissed her ... afterwards, he pulled out his finger and kissed her lips.

It was not the right season for grafting. But both the pear and peach trees survived. It was a miracle. It constantly bothered the youth. Even after he had left his hometown far behind it still lingered in his mind. During his whole youth he paid attention to the development of these two trees. After all, they were the products of an act against nature, and their continued development was definitely a violation of natural law. The pear tree never flowered or bore fruit. Its branches grew crazily in all directions and the trunk continued to expand. Seen from a distance, the tree looked like a terrifying dome blotting the sky. The peach tree flowered in the flowering season. It was very beautiful, blood-red flowers seemed to be dripping from the branches. Its unendurable splendour was very unsettling to passersby; they quickened their pace to get as far away from it as possible. One year it bore its only fruit. This peach was the colour of the flowers and enormous. Everyone saw the monstrosity, and no one dared touch it. The youth had already grown into a man. He called forth his courage and took a bite of the strange fruit. When he finished eating it, he headed out on his journey.

I met my cousin a total of three times: the first time was in our hometown; the third time was in the three-bedroom apartment with the iron door; the second time was in that picturesque city.

The next time I saw my cousin was through sheer luck. That year I accepted an invitation to visit a famous mountain. I had to change buses in a city nestled by a river, but I was delayed there for two days because I could not buy a ticket. While waiting I remembered that my cousin was at a vocational school there.

I called her up and went to see her and her family.

Until then I knew very little about my cousin and her life. I remembered that after she graduated from high school she had entered a vocational school, and after graduating she had stayed on at the school. She had married one of her professors, I think it was her class adviser, and she now had a child ... I did not know anything else. I had had no direct contact with her. All the news about my cousin and my uncle had been filtered through various channels before being passed to me. That is not to say it was not accurate; it was just repeatedly simplified so that only the bare facts remained when it reached me. To tell the truth, I could not remember her husband's name, and I also was not sure whether it was "agricultural machinery" or "agricultural technology". Thank heaven in the end I remembered at all.

I bought a map and found the approximate location of the school and boarded a bus heading in that direction. I got off the bus and walked straight ahead. I saw the mountain jutting precipitously overhead. It was dusk, and the dark red sun was setting in the western sky. I watched it for a moment, but decided that it was not so magnificent. It paled in comparison with the sunset my cousin and I had watched from the hillside when we were young.

A man walked towards me. I asked him for directions.

He was a wrinkled old man. He hurriedly, no, dodderingly walked towards me. He must have had some very pressing business. I politely asked him the way to the school. He stopped, but his reactions were slow. I asked him again in a louder voice, and this time he responded. His voice was feeble and unsteady.

He said: "It's right over there."

I turned, crossed the street, and found the white sign with black characters. I entered through the main gate of the school and inquired at the information office. I talked to a woman who had a scar on her lip. When she heard me mention my cousin's name, she examined me very carefully. She looked as if she wanted to ask me something but had suddenly forgotten what it was. Her sewed up mouth hung half open, an expression of curiosity on her face. I asked her again, and she told me the exact location.

I found the squat little house, and I saw the row of squatter shacks. I called for her. My voice contained a myriad of different, complicated elements. A woman came out of one of the shacks. She answered as she came out and walked straight towards me. It was undoubtedly my cousin. I went over to her, trying hard to see in her what I remembered from seventeen years before. We stopped and stood very close to each other. I believed that in our hearts we were both very shocked.

I saw my cousin's son. He was a quiet child. He was just five years old. He did not resemble his mother. I joked with the child, but he acted as if he were only perfunctorily tolerating me. When we were not talking I noticed that a mature, old expression often crossed his face. It puzzled me.

We ate dinner very late. We were waiting for her husband. She said that he had left campus to go to a colleague's apartment to fetch something and that he had not said where he was going to eat. I said: "Don't worry, let's wait for him." We waited a long time, so long that my stomach was rumbling with hunger and the child was beginning to complain. My cousin hesitated. I tentatively guessed her position in this household. The food on the table was getting cold. We decided to eat first.

I had a big appetite that day. My chopsticks moved continuously, and my cousin kept adding food to my bowl. The child sat silently watching the two of us defer to each other. I had just about finished, but my cousin added another piece of lotus root to my bowl. Just then the door opened and a man walked in. My cousin turned her head and then said, "Oh, he's home."

I looked up. I seemed to have seen him before. It was the old man I had stopped to ask directions. How had he become my cousin's husband?

That man headed towards the dinner table. As the face came closer and closer, there was no trace of a smile, only a very strange expression. A curse flashed through my mind: 'Hell, why did you marry such a good-for-nothing?'

When the daughter returned to her parents' home, she wanted to find the confidence and courage to jump out of that bitter sea. Had her mother been at home, the result would definitely have been different. She was very unlucky and returned disappointed.

Her mother had gone to the provincial capital. As she had done several years before, she took with her local delicacies to give to the provincial secretary-general and his wife. This time she had no political injustice to ask them to resolve; she just wanted to express her sincere thanks.

I stood up. The old face was still moving, the strange expression still there. I forced a smile.

My cousin said, "This is my ..."

He waved his hand to cut her off and asked me directly: "Who are you?"

I said: "I am her cousin."

Again he asked: "Who are you?"

Again I thought his reactions too slow, just like when I stopped him on the street. I said loudly: "I am her cousin."

He did not say anything. His eyes looked hazy and unclear. He stared at me for a long time. Slowly, he let out a smile. But the smile was insincere and somewhat sinister. I saw my cousin shiver.

I put down my chopsticks. I said: "I am her cousin. He," I pointed to the boy, "Should call me uncle."

She had surrendered to his despotism. Only in her heart did she secretly curse him, "You bastard!" He would yell and scream and brazenly use that ugly woman for his stimulation and his pleasure. She could not understand in what way she was inferior to the woman with the scar on her lip. In his heart she and the ugly woman had changed position. It was very unfair. There was no one else who saw her that way. It was very cruel, what he did to her, as if he had taken a file and filed away at her beating heart. She had aged dramatically. Her strength was almost completely exhausted. Her whole body was numb and cold, hard and stiff like a machine. She knew that it was a machine that belonged to him, like his teacup, his towel ... any of his other things. When he needed it he would use it. He never considered that this thing had its own life. It really was like this. But at the same time this thing had a kind of flexibility: Whether or not he used it, to him it contained no life. At these times, her soul drifted away, leaving behind an empty shell with which he could do what he pleased.

His wife started to resist. She drew strength from her cousin.

One day she had a revelation: the image of that twelve-year-old boy that had remained in her heart was not at all accurate. Many years had passed, and he had certainly grown into a man. He was the same age as that man in front of my eyes. How did her cousin's appearance compare to that man's?

Just then the man screamed at the top of his lungs.

She said: "Yes, you are the same age as my cousin."

When she had finished speaking, a surge of pleasure filled her heart. She felt as if a drop of spring water had accidentally fallen on her dry, parched lips, refreshing and invigorating her. But clearly it was far too little to quench her thirst. It was as if she had suddenly seen a majestic, strange mountain and now she were standing at its base. She was bewitched. She wanted to discover the source of that sweet spring water. She wanted to explore all the strange scenery of that bizarre peak ...

He gasped. His murky eyes still stared at her. He despised her.

She looked at his horrible face. She saw his defeat, his inferiority. She knew that the explanation for their simultaneous aging was incorrect. Her transformation was a superficial one that had occurred under the influence of an outside force. But his was an inherited, irresistible metamorphosis of his life itself.

He had conserved enough energy to jump and hit her. She did not utter a sound. He gnashed his teeth and beat her viciously ... when he had vented most of his anger, he began to lust after another kind of outlet.

She accepted the challenge. He was silent. She had turned into a lifeless machine. He secretly reminisced; from the bottom of her heart she called out. He yelled out for that woman; she just said: Cousin, cousin ..."

In the end the husband compromised, but with himself, not with his wife. He compromised with his desires. He was never able to beat them. Outwardly they still appeared as husband and wife. It was not an overt agreement. It was a silent admission, a result of their battles from which neither emerged victorious. She understood that there was no way her husband would leave the matter at that. In his hatred he wanted revenge — and not just towards his wife.

The old face grabbed a chair, then hesitated and put it down. He picked up a plate, then again hesitated and put it down. In the end, he grabbed a small dish and threw it at me.

That small dish flew in an arc and brushed past my face.

I looked on in a kind of enjoyment as I watched him complete these actions. I saw through him. He was a cowardly, narrow-minded, slightly clever man. When he lifted up the chair and then put it back, he did it because he feared seriously injuring me. He put down the big plate for the same reason. He threw that small plate at my face because he wanted to leave a mark of my humiliation.

I lowered my head and the dish flew past. It shattered on the concrete floor a metre behind me.

I decided it was time for me to strike. I wanted to push back the table and smash all the plates and dishes on that old face. I did not do that. I walked around my cousin, around the dinner table, and slowly crossed over to him.

Just as we began to fight, someone came in and tried

to break us up. It was a woman. I recognized the woman. She was the one from whom I had asked directions at the information office, the one who wanted to say something and then stopped herself. I looked at my cousin and the fierce expression on her face and then spat on the ground.

I found the scar on that woman's lip. I shouted at her: "Get the hell out of here!"

I kicked the door closed. I grabbed him by the neck. That pale, terrified old face was very close to mine. I asked him: "What do you want me to do with you? Should I break your neck? Should I split you in two?"

I released my grip. He crumpled to the floor.

I opened the door and picked him up again. I yelled: "Go and get your friends and bring them back to fight. Go and find your boss and bring him back to get even with me!" I hurled him out through the door and then kicked it closed. Then I turned and looked at my cousin.

I said: "Talk! Tell me everything!"

When the daughter returned home she wanted to pour out all her bitterness. She was unable to do what she wanted. Unfortunately, her mother had gone to the provincial capital.

Her mother went to the house of the provincial secretary-general. She carried with her local delicacies to give as gifts. As soon as she had dropped off the presents she left. She did not have any favours to ask of them, she only wanted to express her heartfelt thanks.

Her mother said farewell to the secretary-general and his wife. The wife told her to return often. She walked past the neatly trimmed winter trees, she walked out of the arched doorway in the garden wall, she walked through the garden-style provincial government compound, she passed by the small red building with the distinctive architecture and the spiral staircase, she walked past the guard standing at attention ... Her mother did not stop at the train station. She continued on to the long-distance bus station. She pulled out the last coins from her wallet and bought a bus ticket.

Her mother did not know that her married daughter was waiting at home.

Because she was short of money, her mother took a long-distance bus home. In normal circumstances she would have arrived home four hours later than if she had taken the train. But when the bus was thirty-five kilometres from the provincial capital, it crashed through the guard-rail of a bridge and plunged headfirst into the heart of a river twelve metres deep.

She started to tell her cousin everything. As she talked she hugged her child. She told him everything, the beginning, the middle, and the end. She began with her mistake at the college entrance exam, she told him about the class monitor's joke, the dates involving three people, the elaborately woven trap. She told him how she had willingly walked into the trap for her material benefit. She told him about her husband's dismembering of her wedding dress, she told him about his calling for that other woman ... she told him all the details she should have told her mother, no matter how embarrassing they were. She told him everything. Her emotions gradually calmed down and she recited in a dispassionate voice as if she were reading from a book, telling a fanciful story which had no connection with herself. It was frightening. She described a terrible disaster, a picture of hell.

She finished. Her cousin was smoking, one cigarette after another. It seemed as if he too had walked into hell.

When her cousin opened his mouth he sounded as if he were passing judgement. He said: "As to your family, as to your child, as to your parents' wishes that their married daughter should not divorce ... strictly speaking, these are all weights, they are all curses. Of course, there are some things in life which are very difficult to stamp out: using these weights to guarantee a relative balance, using the curses to create an existence running counter to reason and emotions ... the key is to see through these things and understand that they are weights and curses. They will immediately become insignificant and powerless ... the key is to eliminate the disaster, save yourself, and walk out of hell."

It was the middle of the night. No, it was already almost dawn.

Her cousin said: "Cousin, you are right. You must do it this way. I support you."

Her voice was dispassionate, but her descriptions were nonetheless terrifying. She had described a picture of hell. Her cousin was deeply affected. Later, they began to discuss the situation.

The topic was itself flexible and could embrace many other things ... in 1937 a superior student was chased and beaten by his classmates; twenty years later there was a big-character poster with the title "Please Do Not Allow Your Wife To Meddle In Politics"; that same year a group of rightists wrote a letter from a mine on a mountain; twelve years later there was the internal strife among the people; another twelve years later there was a struggle between vocational students about to graduate ... and there was also man's ability to endure, even in the face of lust, enticement, and long-term violence.

The cousins had not thought of all these things. They only had a narrow discussion about the matters in hand.

A key moved in the lock in the door. I straightened up. Sure enough, that old face walked into the room. He was still alone. He closed the door with a thud. Then he came and knelt in front of me.

He said: "Cousin, uncle ... it's all been a misunderstanding. Please don't tell anybody. It was a complete misunderstanding. We are all relatives. Just forget about it."

I looked at him suspiciously.

He spoke very fluently, not at all in his usual unconfident manner. He seemed to be reciting well-rehearsed lines. What was going on?

I understood. His goal was very clear: he was purposely starting a quarrel to make me, such a contrast to his old and ugly self, never want to return to this household. Afterwards, everything here would be in his hands and he could return to his former role as master.

Therefore he knelt down in what he thought was some sort of victory pose.

The second time the cousins saw each other was seventeen years later. The situation in which they met was not as wonderful as it was the first time they were together. Just before he left, he told his cousin to come to him for help at any time. He drew her a map of the route and gave her a key to his three-room apartment.

The three-room apartment had an iron door, so no one could disturb them. It was the middle of the night. The man who lived in that apartment went into the study. That night his cousin was staying in that room.

As soon as she had said goodbye to her cousin, she entered into a life-and-death struggle in which she paid an extremely heavy price; she sacrificed her reputation, her child, her father's love ... her opponent turned these into knives which he threw at her one after another. She gave up everything a woman can abandon. In the end, she was victorious.

Even during the most difficult periods she did not go to her cousin for help. She did not use the map or the key to the three-room apartment. She carried the heavy burden alone.

In the middle of the night in the study of a three-room apartment, two people held each other tightly. The thin, withered person kept talking, talking, talking....

Their identities changed again. He was not her husband, he was not her class adviser; she was not his wife, she was not his student. Objectively speaking, the two were colleagues. They were, of course, also enemies.

The household was now divided in two. He and the child lived in the small house. She lived in the shed that had previously been the kitchen.

They still had ties: the child. The child still chased

around, calling out "Mum". She cooked for the child and washed his clothes.

Later, she moved to a room on a different part of the campus. It was still a single room, but the conditions were somewhat better. Out of compassion and a sense of justice, the school had taken special care of her.

The woman appeared every day on campus, hurrying back and forth. She still wore that dress. Perhaps it was out of habit, perhaps she felt constrained by her status as a divorced woman, or perhaps she had lost confidence in her withered and transformed body.

The woman spent all her free time before and after work in her little room. She silently pondered the past, re-examining every episode. When she removed herself from the situation and took a bird's-eye view of events, she was full of admiration for her endurance. If she had to do it all over again, there was simply no way she would be able to. Slowly, she became aware of another aspect: the whole story sounded so unreal. Even though she herself had experienced it, when she related the details people regarded it as just another cheap, melodramatic story written to take advantage of the common people.

There was another metaphor: the story resembled a very tight chain. If there had been any chance occurrences, any errors, the chain would have broken and ceased to exist.

The mother had not seen her son for a long time. Before he would secretly run over to see her, but now he came less and less often. Then she stopped seeing him altogether. After asking around she heard that he had gone to his grandparents' home. Two years later, he reappeared on campus. He was dark and countrified. She waited patiently, but he never came to look for her. He had already started school. One day she stopped him and called to him. He looked frightened and did not know who she was. She came closer and he ran away. Several days later, he saw her again and cursed her, calling her a "sorceress", and throwing stones at her ... she sobbed for a long time. She knew it was that hateful man's revenge.

But that was only the overture.

Within less than six months the man remarried. The new wife had also been a former student of his. She had a scar on her lip and had been his next-door neighbour. There was a brief period of courtship, but they had not been together for very long. It had been sparked off by a chance discussion. The divorced woman had already moved out. The next-door neighbour came in and asked why they had divorced. She suspected that the cousin had been the cause of the marital problems. She had heard of the cousin. That day when he had asked for directions at the information office, she knew who he was. She was obviously shocked. He looked ten years younger than he really was, and had a look that made women's heart beat fast. The two men were the same age, but they were diametrically opposite. She knew what was going to happen, and to tell the truth, she hoped it would happen. She told her former class adviser about his arrival. She said: "Your wife's cousin has come. Do you know you are the same age? You would not know it by looking at him!"

Things did not turn out as she expected ... her former class adviser was not interested in mulling over the past. He told her frankly that he could not get excited about his ex-wife. He said that the only times his passion was aroused was when he thought of her.

She was greatly moved. Perhaps she had felt long ago that it would end like this. She ran into his arms, saying she wanted to marry him.

The woman next door had a husband. He was a worker at the school. He was a timid and weak-willed man. She quickly got an amicable divorce from him and he moved into the shack across the way. She tossed him aside as easily as if she were throwing away old clothes. They knocked down the walls between the two houses and held the wedding there. During the festivities that man hid in the kitchen and peeked his head out to watch. He had turned into a pathetic insect-like creature.

He even attracted the sympathy of his former wife. She said: "You really are stupid. Go and find yourself another woman and set up a new family."

After my cousin's marriage had fallen apart, for a time she did not plan to start a new one. She wanted to be alone for at least five years before finding a new home. But after just two years she put a "seeking marriage" notice in the newspaper. There were just a few responses and they all came from men of very low calibre.

The divorced woman was soon pestered by a suitor. This man had formerly been her next-door neighbour. He was an uneducated worker at the school. He was always following her around eavesdropping on her and writing garbled love-letters to her in crooked handwriting. He was a weak-willed and timid man, so unquestionably someone had put him up to it. One day, in front of a crowd of onlookers, she loudly and severely rejected him.

She had peace for only a few days before he once again got up his courage. This time he used another method. He stood for the whole night outside her door. He had hoped that the scene people had described to him would really occur: she would be unable to resist the torment of his love, and would rush out and throw herself into his arms. She was awake all night. She heard his fingers scratching against the door. She leapt out of bed, threw open the door, grabbed a stick and charged out. There was nobody there. The troublemaker had run off, leaving nothing but the boundless night.

She was alone and helpless. She needed to save herself once again.

After the cousins parted for the second time they did not stay in touch. She did not want to bother him. The second time they met had been embarrassing enough. One day she went to his apartment and spent the night there. She went there simply because she needed a place to stay; she had gone to the provincial capital for another reason.

Things were not so good in the new household with its expanded living space. There was still the same old problem: his character was old and weak. There was nothing the woman with the scar on her lip could do. Fortunately the new couple quickly transferred their interests. For a long time, the light in the house stayed on deep into the night. The two of them were going through stacks of letters from men responding to a "seeking marriage" notice. The wife had brought the letters back from the information office. They were very experienced at this kind of work. They used a warm towel to open the envelopes, skimmed the contents, and then divided them into two piles. They burned the larger pile. They resealed the envelopes in the smaller pile and the next day the woman with the scar on her mouth took them back to the information office and then delivered them to the addressee.

It was the middle of the night. No, it was almost dawn. The withered person was still talking, talking ...

My cousin wanted to start a new family so she placed a "seeking marriage" notice in another newspaper. She received a few letters, but after she opened them she was greatly disappointed: if it was not from an illiterate peasant then it was from some chronically ill old man, or a middle-aged widower with a lot of children, or a paraplegic ... unwittingly she had entered into a realm of despair, and was on the verge of a nervous breakdown. Just at this time, a response came from the provincial capital that greatly surprised her.

The light in the house stayed on until the middle of the night. The couple were still going through letters responding to the "seeking marriage" notice. This task was unavoidably dull and they quickly grew tired of it. They wanted to do something completely different, to add a little excitement ... they decided on a hoax.

My cousin read the letter from the provincial capital over and over. That man was thirty-two, 1.75 metres tall, a college graduate, a secretary in a provincial-level office, he had an apartment with two bedrooms and a hallway, a kitchen and a bathroom; and he had no parents or any other burdens. There was a picture of a normal-looking, educated man. The letter said that he had already been secretly to her school and seen her. He stressed that he was not responding out of pity or sympathy. He really did love her. After they married she could transfer to a comfortable position in a vocational school attached to his office. In the letter he said he wanted her to come to the provincial capital so they could meet. He was a very meticulous person. He described in great detail the place where they were to meet. The time was very flexible. He added that because his work was so busy and might be unable to get away, if on the first day he was unable to meet her, would she please return on the second day to wait for him at the appointed place. He really stood head and shoulders above the rest.

My cousin had no choice. Such good luck was rare __ perhaps if she passed it by she would never again have such an opportunity. She had to grasp it while she could.

My cousin rushed off to the provincial city at the appointed time.

It was impossible to define the form of the trap ... it was recognisable, it was part of something frequently seen in life, it was ubiquitous and eternal. On the road of human life these things are unavoidable. Once the trap exists, it pursues one relentlessly, following along in one's shadow. Unless ...

It receded. In 1937 there was a group of students looking for a fight; twenty years later there was a big-character poster; that same year a group of rightists on a mountain wrote a letter; twelve years later the two cousins met; in that same year there was a man tending a flock of geese; twelve years later there was a mistake on the mathematics section of a test; there were the three-person dates; there was the man who at his wife's behest issued clear instructions about two letters twenty-four years apart … It receded.

When my uncle's political case was being re-examined, it encountered unforeseen difficulties: the name register that he had copied by hand was destroyed during the "cultural revolution". A colleague told me this the year I was working in the "rectification" office. At the time he was in charge of such work. I quickly returned to my hometown. The situation was really quite thorny. Everyone knew that the register had existed, but no one could say clearly what it really was. The tutor with his staff, robe, and sunglasses was, along with his contemporaries, long dead. The witnesses were the ones who had got him into trouble by informing on him. Luckily, I had two magic weapons: a directive from the illustrious and powerful provincial secretariat, and my previous foreboding.

I went to see the rehabilitated rightists and said: "Your troubles have arrived."

Of course they recognised me. They knew who my uncle was, and they knew that my career had taken off as quickly as his. They also knew that I had a much greater future ahead of me than my uncle had ever had. When they saw the directive from the provincial secretary-general, they were stunned and for a moment at a loss for words. They incoherently cursed their base and shameless actions. They explained that when they wrote that letter they had wanted only to achieve two goals. They did not think that their superior classmate would suffer so much or for so long, and they had expected trouble to once again fall on their heads.

I said: "Fortunately the matter has fallen into my hands — perhaps it is a lucky chance for all of you to extricate yourselves completely!"

They sighed, and, in accordance with my wishes, no, in accordance with what actually happened that year, they rewrote their statements.

The two people in the study talked until dawn ... At exactly eight a.m., the man accompanied the woman to the meeting point. It was on the bank of the river that encircled the city. Spanning the river was a bridge with nine arches. A road crossed the bridge and headed off towards the horizon. There was a statue. They sat behind a nearby tree, pretending to be engaged in conversation. Their eyes kept looking in that direction, looking to see if a cultured, normal-looking man had appeared. The man was certain that the respondent did not exist. The woman half believed and half doubted. The two were extremely patient. They waited until five o'clock in the afternoon. The statue in front of them was of Meng Jiangnu.* Her miserable,

---

*Meng Jiangnu was a legendary woman of the Qin Dynasty. Her husband was recruited to build the Great Wall and died there. Meng Jiangnu waited in vain for her husband to return. She started a long journey and cried all the way to the Great Wall in search of her husband.

tragic story had been passed down for more than a thousand years, remaining always in the minds and hearts of mankind. It was a everlasting story whose objective constantly changed with present-day requirements. Still, it was only a story. The woman had never actually existed.

The woman arrived in the provincial capital. She carried with her the reply to her "seeking marriage" notice. She arrived at the appointed place at the appointed time. She had already experienced much suffering in her life and had become extremely patient. She even waited until dark, past the agreed time limit of five o'clock. She very much appreciated that man's thoughtful postscript to his letter. No doubt he had pressing business which prevented him from getting away. She did not stay in an inn; she planned to return to her cousin's, spend the night there, and then return the next day to continue waiting.

In the middle of the night, her cousin went into the study where she was staying. She could see in his eyes his excitement and his desire. She was unclear as to the nature of these things, but she understood what he wanted to do. She was confused, feeling that she had no rights to refuse. Of course, as predicted, she was satisfied as she had never been before.

Everyone marvelled at the provincial secretary-general's completion of a successful, unblemished career. He could look forward to the treatment accorded to provincial-level officials, and he could move ahead of time into the secretariat building. This was a two-storey garden-style house with a high brick wall. In fact, his feelings were the exact opposite. He saw two problems: he was about to retire, and his wife's temper was growing worse and worse. He believed he was about to enter a lonely, boring, desolate, and stifling old age.

The secretary-general's wife was forever complaining. Her damaged memory gradually recovered. One day, his wife remembered the woman who had come to the door to ask for the resolution of the injustice done to her husband twenty-four years before. After she had sent them gifts the second time, she no longer came to visit them. His wife grumbled: "To begin with I really could not see how ungrateful she was!"

In the middle of the night there were only two people in my three-room apartment: my cousin and I. The two of us were separated by a room with a balcony. I had always believed that something would happen between us. There was some kind of force connecting us. For a long time I was unable to sleep, thinking about that mysterious force. I smoked a cigarette, drank a cup of tea ... suddenly I understood. It was a river. I examined my body carefully. I saw clearly its colour, its essence. It was a river that had flowed from the distant past, from two branches, simultaneously flowing into my blood and hers. It was a river of consanguinity, and it was pulling us together.

I crushed out my cigarette. I walked into the study and into her life.

I said to her solemnly, "Cousin, we — "

One afternoon just before closing time, a man and a woman entered the Marriage Registry Office. The registrar patiently attended to them. The two had all the necessary documents and credentials. The registrar had just about gone through all of the formalities when he suddenly discovered something. He returned the documents and credentials to them.

He opened a book, pointed to it and said, "Here, chapter two, article six, section one." *

They tried to explain, tried to give examples and reasons to convince him that he should change his mind.

The worker was unable to make any decision, and anyway he wanted to leave work early so he could see to some personal business. He said that there was no precedent for this, that he had to ask for instructions from his superior, and that they should return the next day.

The man and the woman did not take a bus home. They walked down the street. They crossed an intersection with a flashing light, they passed the crowds of people, they walked through the lush, verdant area, they walked by the unmoving, lonely statue, they crossed the bridge with nine arches ... when the man passed the bridge he stopped suddenly; the woman had not followed him. She had stayed on the opposite bank.

The man opened his mouth to call to her, but he quickly closed it. She stood on the opposite bank staring at something. He followed her line of vision. She was staring at the western sky. The sun was just setting.

The man saw a scene as beautiful and magnificent as the one he had seen when he was twelve years old: the setting sun was as large as a basket, and its colour was blood-red.

---

*The Marriage Law in China forbids marriage between cousins.

The colour was spreading and gradually dark-
ening…. The real world had been brazenly usurped
and replaced by an illusion … in an instant, the
bridge with nine arches had disappeared, leaving behind only a red-river.

Two people. One river.

The river stretching between them was the colour of
blood.

Translated by Bill Bishop

Heaven's Course

"Heaven moves on its own course,
It doesn't exist on account of Yao*
Nor perishes on account of Jie**."

— Xun Zi***

THE journalist was due at any moment.

When he came, Chief Director Wu had just finished talking to me: "We have discussed it already. You are to be transferred out of the criminal court department to work in another court." As he left he called out: "You can choose any court you want. Think it over carefully."

I went to see Party Secretary Lu. I wondered what Wu's true motives were. One must be prepared for all eventualities. Transferring from the criminal court to another court was a step downwards. You keep stepping downwards and you fall into a mud pit and can't get yourself out. I spoke to Lu about my misgivings. He was surprised: "You mean to say, you don't want to leave the criminal court?" I nodded.

"Talk about it later," he said. "There's another

---

*Yao, a legendary ruler of ancient China.

**Jie, despotic emperor of the Xia Dynasty.

***Xun Zi (Hsun Tse), 313-230 BC, philosopher of the Warring States Period.

assignment here. A reporter has come to investigate a matter, it might be a criminal case, you're in charge. Keep him company, and cooperate with him as best you can. If there are any problems, come and tell me immediately."

The journalist's name was Hao. He was very young, wore glasses and was slimly-built . He was on the steps of the hotel, standing straight as a flagpole. A ray of afternoon sunlight glinted on his glasses. He had the look of a person who was determined to get to the bottom of things.

As I greeted him, he interrupted me saying: "Don't address me as 'Journalist Hao'. Actually, I'm not a journalist." He took my hand, and appeared to me to be a modest and amiable young man.

He had come secretly to the county, so no-one knew of his arrival until he was unable to find a hotel room for that night. A convention was being held and all the hotels were full. As it grew dark, he reluctantly took out his identification and of course the situation suddenly changed. Even Secretary Lu took time out from the convention to personally escort the journalist to the hotel by car, waving away Hao's protestations about not being a real journalist. Lu just laughed, and thought that the young man was worried the hotel might be too expensive. "We have a rule," he said. "Journalists who come to cover a story live in hotels and everything is free of charge."

Secretary Lu's face exhibited a rare look of caution and he whispered to me: "This man is too modest, too unassuming. You had better be extra careful. The more they are like this, the deeper they are about looking into matters, so we must do our utmost to assist him."

I accompanied Hao through the hotel's splendid glazed-tiled entrance. I had never stayed there before. That night, I slept in an unfamiliar room with scarlet camel wool carpets, oatmeal coloured silk wallpaper, chandeliers and wall lamps. My bed was in the annex, Hao slept in the main bedroom where he tossed and turned throughout the night, as if he wasn't used to sleeping in a strange bed.

Early in the morning, we began our journey to a village called Jianggang.

2

The deputy village head's name was Jiang. He wore a spotless new suit. "I sent out a notice last night," he said. "People who know of the case you are investigating arrived early this morning. We can start the meeting whenever we want."

I remembered coming to this place a couple of years ago when I had to arrest a female bigamist whose name was Hu Youxiang. All I could see then was the desolate landscape. We had a bumpy ride there and Hao's face was as white as a sheet. Yet, in spite of the desolation, this poor village's soil had yielded a startling miracle: though the local government offices were a row of shabby one storey buildings, the village's elementary school next to them was a splendid, high-walled building.

A classroom was taken over for the inquiry. The six people who knew about the case were farmers. Even though the case under investigation had taken place eight years ago, they still remembered as if it were yesterday. ''The government was wise, it eradicated the harm to its people." They all spoke, their meanings were garbled. "He is guilty of the most heinous crime."

The person being denounced had been executed eight years before. His name was Jiang Xiaolan, a sophisticated sounding name filled with poetic and artistic connotations, but when it was the name of a fellow with an evil reputation, it made you feel that something had gone wrong somewhere.

"When the police came to the village, we all breathed a sigh of relief," the farmers recalled. "Each family even thought of letting off firecrackers in celebration, but when we saw that the wrong person was being taken away, our hearts turned cold again."

It seemed as if the farmers lacked the educational background to understand what names meant in this case and spoke as if they had been eating fish but had swallowed a mouthful of bones instead.

Jiang Xiaolan had incurred the wrath of a farmer who was robbed by him eight years ago when he was on his way to town to buy medicine for his sick wife. Xiaolan had reeked of alcohol and stumbling beside him were another couple of drunkards.

"They robbed me of my money and kowtowing to them didn't do any good. I begged them to leave me enough money to get home, but they just took all my clothes and kicked me in the behind."

The journalist was carefully taking notes. Once in a while he glanced at me. I was seated by the window, outside was the quiet and empty school playground. A piece of empty land surrounded by four buildings of classrooms. By the main entrance was an exquisitely inscribed piece of calligraphy. On the peak of the main pillar by the gate a bright red flag fluttered in the blue sky.

The six witnesses signed their names. I read through the document and saw the record was complete. It included all the details of the verdict that was reached that year. Actually the matter was not very complicated. Xiaolan in his early years was arrested for theft. After he came out of prison, he had become a vicious hoodlum. He and his gang roamed the countryside causing trouble everywhere. Nobody had any peace. Once when drunk, he had stopped this farmer to make fun of him, taken his money and his clothes and then let him go, leaving him only his shorts. When the farmer reported the crime, the police came but arrested the wrong man and it was only after a whole month that the mistake was discovered. There had been a mix-up with the names. About the same time the country was involved in a movement called "heavy sentences, quick handling."* Xiaolan was sifted out as the most wanted and became the first to be executed.

The farmers believed that it was heavenly justice that the wrong man was arrested first so that when the "heavy sentences, quick handling" came into operation, Xiaolan paid the ultimate penalty. "If he had been captured earlier he would only have got five years in jail. Instead he got caught at the right time, stuck onto the barrel of a gun and eliminated," the farmers reasoned.

---

*The delay in Xiaolan's capture put off the sentencing of his case. So it happened that this caused his trial to be held after the policy of "heavy sentences, quick handling" was set.

The sky turned to dusk, yet people's opinions had not been fully expressed. The village deputy looked at the journalist and announced an adjournment. Dinner was served late, but was very sumptuous. There was a gloomy mood, for Hao did not even glance at the best meat dishes. He gulped down a bowl of plain rice, put down his chopsticks and left the room. When we returned to the hotel, he made it clear that from the next day, we would get our own meals.

"This is the custom," I said placatingly. "It has always been like this."

"You want to give me problems?" he asked.

I changed the subject, and asked what he thought of the Xiaolan case. He looked over the file and returned it.

"The inquiry was very successful, everyone told the truth," he said. "The records and files are also complete and present a full picture of the case but," he let out a long yawn. "But this isn't the case I want to investigate."

3

It was quite another case he was interested in. This case also took place eight years ago. The events were quite simple. A schoolmaster called Jiang Guangfu rode a bus into the city to buy teaching materials. On the bus he bumped into an acquaintance, who was sitting next to a policeman. The headmaster passed a cigarette over. He was unaware that the acquaintance was in custody and that the policeman was his escort. There was an argument and as a result, Jiang Guangfu was detained for 15 days. He was rearrested as soon as he was released and charged with obstructing an officer in carrying out his duty and insulting behaviour. He was sentenced to 15 years in a labour corrective farm, where he was still now.

"Ay," I said, "there are so many cases, why did you have to pick this one?"

"Oh really?" Hao said. For a long time he stared at me, making me feel I was a blockhead who only made stupid remarks.

That night I twisted and turned on my bed. When it was past midnight, I crept out and phoned Secretary Lu at his home. He sounded sleepy, but when he heard my voice, he immediately became alert.

"He came to investigate the Jiang Guangfu case?" he said. "What's behind it? What's his background?"

I answered that this was still unclear.

"Don't worry," Lu said. "Do your best to help him clear up this case, and get to the bottom of things."

The two of us lived in the village guest house and bought meals in the cafeteria. When I went to the men's room I bumped into the village deputy head. He sighed and said: "It's so hard to serve these people above us. This time it's been rough on you, Judge Chen." He took advantage of when we weren't in the room to place some expensive wine, a bag of peanuts, and tinned fish there.

The village deputy sent people down several times to notify Xiaofeng — the man who had been wrongfully arrested — to come to the local office. He was important to the journalist's investigation of the headmaster's case. We waited three days but didn't see a sign of the man. The village deputy came to the

guesthouse, looked at us with both his hands out-
stretched. "This Xiaofeng, wasn't visiting his relatives
as we originally thought," he said. "He's working in
a construction engineering team in another village."

Hao asked for the address.

"Actually, they're just a bunch of intinerants, they
wander around," he answered. "Some say Hainan,
some say Xinjiang, who knows?"

After lunch, as I was preparing to rest, Hao walked
in. "The inquiry that we·attended the other afternoon
confused me. Why did they hold it?" he asked.

"The execution of Xiaolan was a joyous event. It
was also the village's only noteworthy case," I said.
"When the village deputy heard that a journalist had
come to investigate a case, he naturally thought it was
that one. He is only a government employee on a con-
tract, he doesn't have much knowledge, so he's anxious to prove himself."

Hao sat down without comment. I faced him and
saw the fine hair above his lips. For a second, I felt
envious of one so young and enthusiastic.

Later, we drank the bottle of expensive wine and
gorged on the peanuts and tinned fish. His face gradually turned bright red, even the rim of his eyelids were
red. I probably wasn't much better and blurted out:
"I do have a clue. Just by accident when I was
investigating an bigamist case some years ago, the accused woman was on that same bus."

4

Jiangdian village looked the same in the midst of
spiralling coils of mist. I recognised the adobe huts

with the grass roofs. It had hardly changed. Only when we got to the western part did the village look different. A brick and tile building stood out very clearly. I knocked on the door and called: "Does Hu Youxiang live here?" When a woman opened the door, I said: "We have something to ask her."

"I am she," she said. I hardly recognised her as the person we were looking for. She, however, immediately recognized me. "Aren't you Secretary Chen from the criminal court?"

"At first I thought you were her sister," I replied.

"People who see me again always make this mistake," she laughed. "I don't have any siblings. You knew that when you were investigating my case eight years ago." She glanced behind me: "Hasn't Judge Wu come? Don't both of you work on cases together any longer?"

Judge Wu, of course, was now the Chief Director. Eight years ago, he had commented: "This woman has the makings of a beauty. Her figure, features are all good. Too bad she married the wrong man; it has made her face a pale vegetable colour, a beautiful flower wilted just like that."

His description had been accurate. Eight years ago when I came to the village, I had knocked on the door of a low grass-roofed hut and a woman leant on the door frame like a wilted flower or precious jade damaged. She bowed her head submissively twice when I asked her name. Village officials had accompanied me as I read the warrant for her arrest and handcuffed her.

That was the year in question when she was on the bus where the headmaster and the policeman had the argument. She had witnessed everything.

She looked younger than before. Her skin was full and white, her complexion rosy, with a look of serenity. Were we in a different place, I would have placed her among the educated city dwellers.

"Come in, come in," she said warmly.

The house was spacious. It was made up of three one-storey buildings, a surrounding wall, and a large courtyard in the centre. We heard a "ti-ti-ta-ta" sound. Two of the houses had been converted into one by knocking down the wall between them. Young women were working at rows of sewing machines. Two young men were in the south facing office drinking tea.

This was a small, privately-owned clothing workshop, and the whole building belonged to Hu Youxiang.

Eight years ago when I took her into custody, and walked past a desolate field, she had cried non-stop like an injured pet; a village girl frightened out of her wits. I never thought she would have become such a strong personality and be the mistress of such an establishment.

As I took her out of the village, I removed the handcuffs and told her not to be afraid. "When the time comes," I said trying to console her, "just have a good attitude, and things will be better for you. Who knows, you may never be charged."

I never thought that eight years later, because of another case, I would see her again.

Her parents had married her off to a man from another village, but unfortunately they became ill and died soon after. She had a son and daughter and in the beginning they were not too badly off. Sometimes, the husband had enough money to send back and every year went back to his family for a month or two. But gradually he stayed away longer and longer until for three years she had no news of him. She asked people to write letters for her to find out his whereabouts but they fell like rocks into the sea.

She worked hard in the fields bringing up the two children but her health gave out, having never been very good since the birth of the second child. One day as she was on her way to the fields, she bumped into the local beggar called Gou'er, curled up fast asleep outside the village. She kicked him and said: "Wake up, you lazy-good-for-nothing. Why can't you give a woman some help?"

Whether she ever had an affair with Gou'er was a moot point, but it gave rise to gossip in the village. He was an orphan and had been a beggar all his seventeen or eighteen years. Hu Youxiang made him clean himself up and put on her husband's clothing, which changed his appearance making him more human. As her husband had deserted her, she said, she might as well have Gou'er.

He stayed with her for about ten days and then moved out, but word reached the ears of her husband and this man, who had left his wife and children without a word for three years, accused her in court of bigamy!

She was sentenced to two years in prison.

When we entered her room, the journalist immediately sat down and came straight to the point. Youxiang's face remained expressionless. "Why ask me?" she said. "What does this schoolmaster have to do with me?"

"You were on the bus that day."

"Really?"

I could remain silent no longer: "Eight years ago you accidently spoke of this matter. The villagers helped pay for your fare to Ningxia to find your husband. You got on a bus to the railway station. It was March 15; there's only one bus every day from Jianggang village to the city."

She nodded and admitted that I had a good memory.

"This matter we are investigating happened on that bus," I added. "It conerns a passenger whose name was Jiang Guangfu and a policeman. You might not have known these two people, but you must have seen them quarrelling. How did it start?"

She answered: "I know Jiang Guangfu, he was my teacher. When I was in elementary school I listened to his speech. We all admired him, he could talk for two whole hours without stopping."

5

The name now rang a bell with me. He had been the head of that well-built school in the centre of the village. He had only been in this remote village for two years but the high educational standards were due to his hard work. A remarkable man by any standards.

The precise details of his arrest and imprisonment I was never quite clear about. It had been a busy time for everyone, especially regarding the execution of that arch criminal Xiaolan and his gang.

Fate plays funny tricks. On the day in question the headmaster almost didn't make it to the bus. It had already started driving away, but the driver stopped when he heard him shouting. He hadn't sat down immediately but stood on the step and began lecturing the passengers as if he was in school instructing his flock. The passengers listened patiently for a while and then someone told him to hurry up but he continued talking loudly and gesticulating. Hu Youxiang remembered that the quarrel was an anticipated result: the headmaster had annoyed the majority of the passengers but none thought it would be with the policeman.

"If he had taken his seat and not said a word like everyone else, then it would have been fine," she said. "That day he had a sum of money in donations for the school, so he was very happy and full of himself and was dying to tell everyone. During the whole trip, he kept looking around for someone to talk to."

I felt the same as her. My impression of the teacher had not been a good one. I had experienced his glib speech-making when I was still a secretary and part-time bailiff. When I was in charge of the court, the atmosphere among the spectators seemed different from normal. A dark, middle-aged man was causing trouble in the crowd. He was raising his head and lifting his arms, unusual actions because normally people like that were relatives or had powerful connections with the accused. When one meets this kind of situation, no one can guarantee the result. It made all the muscles in my body tense, as if someone was ready to fire a gun into the air. When the trial was over, a group of people gathered round the man and I went over to listen. He was passing judgment on the trial, from the chief magistrate's attitude, the jury's expressions, to the public prosecution, the defence and the accused's final statement. The one who was criticised most was the defence lawyer. He said that this person's intellect was too shallow, and that he had prepared his defense very badly. He compared the lawyer to someone who wanted to kill a dog, but only stabbed it in the leg, yet appeared very smug and satisfied with the result.

The man who had made these comments was no other than the school headmaster from Jianggang village. At the time I wasn't too clear about his identity, only that the school in this village had been chosen as a model for the whole province, with a work-study programme. This man couldn't possibly be the head of such a prestigious school.

Afterwards, he was heard to say that if he had been the defence lawyer, the whole verdict would have been reversed, that the standard of the judiciary was too low and he was prepared to become a part-time lawyer.

In the bus, the headmaster had glanced at Hu Youxiang but failed to recognise her as a former pupil of his as so many had passed through his school. He had glanced over the passengers and was disappointed that there was no one to talk to. Xiaofeng, the accused, was sitting to one side but had tucked his handcuffed hands inside his sleeves. A hat concealed his face.

Youxiang said that on the day she didn't go out of her way to greet the headmaster. First because it had been a long time and she thought he wouldn't remember her; and secondly, this was her first journey away from home and she was flustered and a little afraid. When the bus started moving she dozed off.

"I woke up suddenly, when the bus went over a pothole. It knocked off Xiaofeng's hat," she continued. "The headmaster then had a clear look at him and the story of the donations spilled out. He threw a cigarette over to him and that's when the officer picked a quarrel with him.''

She stopped her narrative and called over to the two young men waiting in the room to get some good wine and food. I wondered: does man live like a creature wriggling in a net? So many things are beyond comprehension, yet everything goes according to some mysterious plan. If on the day of March 15 the headmaster had missed the bus, and if Xiaofeng's hat hadn't come off, or if another policeman had been the escort, then maybe he wouldn't have been detained and there wouldn't be these stormy waves and he would be home safe and sound.

6

As we ate, Youxiang ordered the two young men, who seemed as if they had nothing better to do but wait attendance on her: "Get on your motorbike and buy some wine from the city. Find a reliable shop. I want only the Gu-jing kind and also some Moutai if there's any. Make sure it's not a fake.'' She was like a boss of the old days, shouting at her hired labour: "You, buy vegetables and eels, horse-shoe tortoises and turtles, buy live and fresh ones no matter how much they cost.''

Her one-storey flat faced south. Between the bedroom and the office was a reception room, filled with expensive but tasteless ornaments. On the wall facing us hung her business licence. On the side there was a blown-up coloured picture of her. There was just this one photograph of herself and no one else. I wondered what had become of the other accused in her case, Gou'er.

As if reading my thoughts she said: "When we were released, Gou'er did suggest we marry, but I had had my tubes tied and couldn't have any more children. I can't expect him to cut off his line of descent."

"How is he now?" I asked.

"Sons and daughters, he has them both — he's not badly off, either. He's the head of an engineering team, and doesn't earn less than I do."

She said she was quite content with her life. "I know what you're thinking," she said frankly. "Women can't do without men. So I hired those two, they're both single; one is five years younger than I am, the other four. I treat them well, they're paid a good salary. Normally they don't have much work to do. You can say I'm paying them for nothing."

Rare and expensive delicacies were put before us. I hesitated but Hao picked up his chopsticks and began eating. She joined us in a drink and grew more talkative. Every time she made a toast she would tell us something about herself. She said when she was a child a blind person told her she would become rich. A couple of years earlier she would never have believed it, but now, it does seem like there's some truth in it.

"The blind person's prediction of wealth is all in my red mole," she said. Because of it, I can live a life of luxury until the end of my days."

The red mole was between her breasts. She started unfastening the buttons of her blouse. The two men serving the food, wrinkled their brows and stared at her, but she ignored them. After she undid three buttons, a bright red, very protruding brassiere was revealed. Fortunately she didn't go any farther but just tugged at her bra and then buttoned up her blouse again.

"Who's to say that what the blind man foretold wouldn't come true?" She emptied her full glass in one go, her eyes swept back and forth over our faces. "If he wasn't so right, would so many things just happen by coincidence?"

Hao gave me a meaningful look. In order to get to the bottom of the Jiang Guangfu case, no matter how far off she wandered, we would have to be patient and listen.

The headmaster had argued with the policeman all the way to the county. When the bus approached the stop, the policeman dragged him off to the Public Security Bureau. She had not gone to watch but had changed buses to get to her destination.

She had seen a train for the first time, that gigantic thing that rumbled and shook the ground beneath one's feet scared her yet she had to stay on this monster for several days and nights. When she thought about it, she couldn't help shuddering.

It was her neighbours who had persuaded her to go to Ningxia. "He is your husband after all. The father of your children." They suggested that Gou'er should move out.

She bit her lip and went to buy a ticket for the train. There was a very long queue in front of the window. After pushing and shoving for four hours she got to the window, only to find when she reached into her pocket to get her money, it was gone. A pick-pocket had stolen the fare the villagers had collected for her.

She threw herself onto the ground, crying bitterly. A kind-hearted traveller gave her the fare home. It was just as well, because her husband had returned to the village.

She rejected his sexual advances and wouldn't let him touch her. Early the next morning, he took their two children and went to the county court to file for a divorce.

The changes in her life in such a short space of time was beyond imagination, from riding the same bus as the headmaster, to the stormy waves afterwards, all in all it was only about two months. It was in the middle of all this public attention that her case took its shape, her sentence decided and her imprisonment.

Chief Director Wu grumbled whenever the case was mentioned: "Who would have thought that this village would have these types of women?" He had been a judge then, and had little sympathy with her hard lot. "In front of you are two roads," he told her. "Either serve two years in prison or repent of your sins here and now and return to your husband."

She chose prison.

Judge Wu was astonished. "You must think it over carefully," he told her. "Prison is no joking matter."

"I made up my mind a long time ago," she shouted. "I want to go to prison!"

He heaved a sigh and she was taken away.

There was an official hearing on the second day but the visitors' seats were empty, no one was interested as it was a civil case. The husband as the plaintiff read out his statement. Hu Youxiang didn't bother to defend herself and accepted all the blame.

"When I said we were together I meant we really lived as a married couple," she said.

This took the husband by surprise, as he expected her to deny the accusation in the hope he wouldn't divorce her. He took the children with him to Ningxia, saying: "I'd like to see how you can get on without me now you are alone."

In his summing up, Judge Wu said: "The husband means what he says, and she prefers prison, then let her go. Maybe it will do her good."

As she recalled the past, she couldn't help getting emotional. She said that her stubbornness at that time was like a sign. "If my case had been delayed I might have changed my mind and been in real misery as a consequence, and not gone to the corrective farm. Then I probably wouldn't have what I have today," she said in thankful tones.

7

She knew the whereabouts of another important character in our Jiang Guangfu case called Xiaofeng. He had indeed joined an engineering team, as the village deputy had surmised but had not gone to Hainan Island or trail-blazing in the wilds of Xinjiang.

"Xiaofeng married into a local family and is one of us," she said. "He wanted to work for Gou'er and asked me to help him out."

Gou'er's team was working about 40 miles away. She suggested we could go over there to enquire, and we'd see. Gou'er's engineering team was quite well known. "But they're very strict," she warned. "If Xiaofeng can't get away, ask for Gou'er."

She was right. We found Xiaofeng, but as he spoke, his eyes kept glancing at his watch and looking behind him. An ugly six-storey building was being constructed. The builders were coating a mosaic-like material on the surface and someone was yelling down from the scaffolding for Xiaofeng to hurry.

He said he had no time to talk as this was a private enterprise and the boss was very strict. He worked 12 hours a day, and the remaining time was spent in eating and sleeping. He suggested we come in winter when building was halted, then he could speak as long as we liked.

"The boss regards time as money," he looked towards the scaffolding, ran a couple of steps and then called back: "If there was a way of paying people according to how long they spoke then that would be marvellous."

The Xiaofeng of eight years ago would not have spoken like this when he was wrongfully imprisoned for a month before being released. He did not utter a word but kowtowed and lay on the ground.

Judge Wu and I had just returned from court and as we walked past the hostel for detainees, we saw someone's bottom raised high in the air. Judge Wu said in rather a patronising tone that some people really should be in a class for illiterates and this particular person kowtowing like mad had been arrested by mistake.

Xiaofeng walked on in front of us from the gate. We were all going the same way. At the bus stop, passengers were getting onto the bus for Jianggang village but

Xiaofeng continued walking in the direction of the village. Judge Wu thought it strange, and asked him why.

"Reporting to the squad leader," Xiaofeng barked out and got on his knees. "I have no money to buy a ticket."

"Look how they have handled matters," Judge Wu grumbled. "They caught the wrong man and then freed him and treated him like a chicken."

He pulled up a teary-eyed, runny-nosed Xiaofeng and gave him five yuan.

When Youxiang told us of Xiaofeng's whereabouts, she also asked us to send greetings to Judge Wu. "My life today is because of him as well as my own efforts. Tell him," she said shaking my hand. "Now he is a director, he must be busy, but he should take some time off and have a meal at my place."

I nodded but was undecided whether to tell Wu of her new life style. In reality she had been quite lucky, when she was sent to a corrective labour farm. She had learned to become a dressmaker and the post-natal problems that had dragged her health down were cured. The official in charge of education fell in love with her and the close relationship helped her to become more self-confident and assertive. By working hard, she became the head of her prison group. She learnt about people and the outside world and decided to make plans for a new life when she was released.

They kept their affair secret for over a year. He was a married man but he was prepared to leave his wife and promised to find a job for Youxiang nearby, so that they could be together permanently. She made no commitments, but when she had her release papers in her hand, she suggested they spend the night in a hotel outside the city. After a night of passionate love-making, she told him: "This has been like a college education and now I've got my diploma. I can go out and start a career." She was no longer a simple country girl and it gave the worldly-wise education tutor a good lesson.

8

Though we were unable to spend too long with Xiaofeng, I found out the reason why Hao first appeared on the scene. The headmaster had written a letter to a well-known journalist appealing for his help. The journalist had thrown the letter into the wastepaper basket where Hao had retrieved it and decided to make his own investigations. "Such simple matters sometimes can have an explosive effect on society," he said.

We found a cheap hotel near the engineering team. It was not at all suitable for people of our calling.

"You're a journalist after all," I said. "Living in a room like this, don't you think its lowering your standards?"

"I told you a long time ago not to call me that," he said solemnly. "Actually, I'm not really a journalist."

I didn't answer. People say the top people have airs, while the lower people benefit. The more costly the food and board, the more people could claim on their expenses, just as Secretary Lu had suggested. I guessed the news agency had allocated a set amount and Hao wanted to save some money and put it in his own pocket. When the receipt was made out, I had the hotel put it on my bill.

Two people in a little room was extremely stuffy. I couldn't sleep so I turned on the light. His eyes were wide open and he looked as if he had a lot on his mind. I asked him how he came down here. It put him on his guard and he became rather evasive before turning off the light. In the dark he admitted that he had this sense of justice, but told me not to have too noble opinion of him.

"Once this case gets known," he said, "it would alleviate my extremely, extremely urgent problem."

Hao happened to be out when the village deputy walked in. "Secretary Lu hasn't been able to reach you for several days, he's a bit anxious," he said. "He wants to know if there are any problems with the investigation."

I replied: "None. Everything's going smoothly."

"He instructed me to tell you," he said, "that besides doing your best to help Hao's investigation, you must boast a little about our handling of the Xiaolan case."

I said: "All right."

I didn't tell Hao of the visit neither did I boast to him about the Xiaolan case. The enquiry that afternoon at Jianggang village I felt was satisfactory enough.

The Xiaolan case was indeed of benefit not only to the local people but also to the two men who had handled the case namely, Secretary Lu and Judge Wu. The day of Xiaolan's execution, the people of Jianggang village let off strings of small red firecrackers to celebrate. Everywhere you could hear the sound of "Pi-pa Pi-pa" and the smell of firecrackers stung one's nostrils.

Xiaolan had thought people were giving him a good send-off and became excited. He refused any support and jumped into the lorry which was taking him to his death. On the way he behaved like a character from a film, with his head raised and chest jutting out, as if he was the hero defending a just cause. He even kicked his fellow criminal who lay paralysed on the ground: "Don't be so chicken!"

When Xiaolan knelt down, he kept looking around him. The executioner straightened his head, there was a "pai!" and his brain exploded into smithereens.

9

The details of the false imprisonment of Xiaofeng instead of Xiaolan was because of the similarity of the two names when written down. The farmer who had been robbed was interviewed by the assistant chief of police whose educational background was a bit lacking. He painstakingly read the complaint and mistook the character "Lan" as "Feng".

The assistant chief issued orders for the arrest. The duty officer was called Luo but Luo was engaged to be married to the daughter of Secretary Lu, so the assistant chief was a little nervous of sending the future son-in-law of his superior to arrest such a dangerous criminal.

"You can have two other men to help you," he said.

"That's unnecessary." Officer Luo drummed his chest: "I'd like to get him on my own."

Officer Luo took the bus to the village. He didn't

use his family connection to get preferential treatment from the village authorities. He asked someone the way to Jiangpu Village and got there by noon. He looked smart in his uniform and the villagers stood outside their doors nervous and excited.

"Where is Xiaofeng?" he asked an old man.

No-one was surprised that he should ask for him before arresting Xiaolan. Xiaofeng was a member of the local militia. He was a strong young man and law-abiding. The villagers thought that as Xiaolan wasn't afraid of the police, and might cause trouble, it was obvious help would be needed.

Xiaofeng was having breakfast when Officer Luo arrived, but he put down his bowl and got up.

"Just sign your name here," Luo said.

Without a second thought, Xiaofeng signed his name and turned round to look for some rope to take with him to tie up Xiaolan. Instead his wrists were grabbed and he was handcuffed.

As we heard about the whole incident from Xiaofeng, we decided perhaps we should take Hu Youxiang's suggestion and look for Gou'er. He was very frank: "Had it not been for you and Judge Wu's help that year, when I was sentenced I would never have had a taste of the world." He sounded like Hu Youxiang. "Where would I be today?"

If we wanted to talk to Xiaofeng for ten days or more, it was fine by him. He would even get his full pay. He didn't mind about the loss of man-hours. As the head of a private engineering team, Gou'er had the right to decide.

Xiaofeng was very calm as he recalled the past, as if it was a story that had nothing to do with him.

"It wasn't Officer Luo's fault," he said. It was hot and even stuffier with three people in the hotel room. He wiped the sweat off his brow and Hao added his statement to his notes.

"I would have also followed the name on that warrent and arrested the man."

Xiaofeng had worn the hat to hide his face after his arrest and when the bus hit the pothole, his handcuffed hands could not keep it on. As a result, the schoolmaster recognised him and yelled out his name.

Xiaofeng had been working in a brick kiln when he first met Jiang Guangfu. The headmaster had taken his students on a work experience course at the kiln as part of the school's curriculum. The fine school building was the result of the headmaster's efforts and the people recognised and appreciated his hard work. Xiaofeng on the other hand was also a hard worker, although not a great talker. He was always willing to give his time and labour in any project that needed doing. That was why the headmaster had tossed a cigarette over to him and it was this cigarette that had started the dispute. On the bumpy bus, it rolled onto Luo's lap. The sleepy policeman saw a dark face smiling in his direction and the cigarette and mistakenly thought it was for him. He put it in his mouth and was about to light it up when the headmaster shouted:

"Hey, the cigarette isn't for you!"

Luo turned bright red but controlled himself and returned the cigarette but all the passengers were looking at this awkward scene with amusement, and as Luo thought about it, he became irate. When the headmaster was about to toss it again in the direction of

Xiaofeng, he made a halting gesture with his hand: "Do you know who this person is?"

The headmaster misunderstood the question, totally unaware that inside Xiaofeng's sleeves his hands were handcuffed. He answered of course he knew who he was and at the same time tossed the cigarette in his direction. Luo intercepted the cigarette in mid-air and threw it out of the window.

Neither man would give an inch.

Nobody tried to mediate, so the two continued quarrelling. Xiaofeng, scared, tried to speak, but the two told him to shut up.

The headmaster shouted: "What's wrong with giving him a cigarette?"

Officer Luo became even more enraged by his tone and shouted back: "You're deliberately trying to impede public security!" He threatened he would charge him. But Jiang Guangfu let out snort of contempt.

"Explain the rules regarding impeding public security," he retorted.

As soon as Luo began to speak, he sneered and said he had got the rules wrong and recited the codes of law and sarcastically consulted Luo about any mistakes. Luo was speechless.

It was just like a lecture on law. The headmaster even referred to many moving and interesting cases as examples and which publication they appeared in. The passengers were most impressed by his eloquence.

Officer Luo sat like a deflated ball and was silent. But, after the bus reached its stop, he suddenly leapt up.

"You have showed off enough of your power and prestige. Now it's my turn." He seized the headmaster by the collar.

10

I told Hao I was going back to the county. He just replied: "All right" and continued browsing through his notes.

"Secretary Lu told me to report on any progress but I haven't kept in touch with him for some time," I said. "He wants to know if you have encountered any problems. I think he also wants to know about your background and reasons for this investigation and what you intend doing afterwards."

"They'll know sooner or later," he replied casually.

"They want to know now," I persisted.

He continued reading his notes. I reminded him of what he said about not having too noble an opinion of him. "It's not easy getting by," I said. "Sometimes you have no choice but to do things that are against your wishes.

He didn't take my hint and said instead: "You've been tired out these days accompanying me, you ought to go back to the county and get some rest. Fortunately I have all the evidence I need so all I need is some peace to finish writing up the report.

He saw me off at the busstop. There were soft and fine hairs above his mouth, and I sighed enviously at his youth. I felt at ease. Even if his attempt for justice failed, there had been no great harm done to him personally.

As the bus drew away, he was still standing on the same spot, waving.

I met Secretary Lu and Chief Director Wu at the

County Secretary's office. The two men stood with their hands behind their backs in the golden ray of light.

Officer Luo entered the room as I began to speak. He looked as if he had been on a long hard journey. Lu motioned him to sit by Wu, and said: "Right, continue with what you were saying."

I told them that it was Jiang Guangfu, the headmaster who had been writing letters everywhere complaining about the labour farm. "He gave names to a journalist called Hao," I said, "which is how this all came about."

Lu said: "Of all people, why did he choose to write to this journalist?"

I lied and said that Hao was responsible for the newspaper column which dealt with injustices and that he had written many articles on similar cases. "Perhaps the headmaster read those articles and then kept his name in mind."

"Just what did that letter say?"

"I didn't see the letter. But listening to Hao, he seemed pretty serious. He said he would get to the bottom of this case. His own words were: to make clear the truth to everybody." I continued lying: "Jiang Guangfu is head of an elementary school. There's ink in his veins and he's used to showing off. He used a lot of words to paint an innocent and pathetic picture of himself. Hao must have been taken in."

"Was it some provincial head that sent him down?"

"I don't think that was the background," I said. "He told me there was another reason for coming here in secret."

"Then it must be hecause he is in charge of the news agency." Lu said. "Otherwise how could he come down to investigate a case without first getting permission?"

I answered it was hard to fathom the minds of literary people. Hao had written quite a few important articles which we didn't happen to see. "I understand well-known journalists don't have to ask for instructions, they can go wherever they please and do whatever they want."

As soon as I spoke I realised I had made a slip and hurriedly said: "I'm sure he is not in authority."

I saw out of the corner of my eye, Officer Luo nodding.

He agreed with me. He had just returned from the provincial capital where although he hadn't got all the facts, he could at least prove that the journalist wasn't anyone important.

"It was bad timing when I went," he said. "They were in the middle of a special event."

He had found the news agency that was on Hao's press card and had gone several times over two days but found the whole building locked up. "It made one wonder whether this was the place where all the lazy people in the world gathered."

On the third day he was lucky. A door was open at the magazine office. A well-made-up girl, with her legs resting on the desk, was reading a newspaper. "Are you a writer submitting a manuscript?" she asked.

She said she had just joined the agency and was responsible for receiving and distributing manuscripts. "No-one is around, they are brewing up a plot at the moment."

Luo was bewildered. The girl, waving her legs, explained: the high-ups had sent an inspection team and the news agency was going to create a new team of managers. All the employees were in the meeting hall of another building and every day they were in serious discussion about people's opinions and other activities. It was rumoured that qualified middle-rank government employees had an equal opportunity to get promotion, so those who were competitive and ambitious were afraid to go home for lunch and even begrudged the seconds for going to the lavatory. When trainee reporters were being considered for a permanent post, they also began to be more punctual.

Luo asked the young woman whether she had ever heard of a journalist called Hao. She said regulations forbade questions being asked about the staff and not even the personnel of the magazine could tell who was who, or the names of those in the agency. She suggested Luo peeped through the glass window of the news agency's door at the list of names on the duty roster.

Although the paper was torn, he could see the name of someone called Hao on it.

"Hao coming at such an unusual time clarifies the situation," Luo said. "He couldn't compete for selection to the new staff, because he isn't an employee of middle-rank."

Secretary Lu wanted me and officer Luo to clear up the question of whether he was sent by the provincial leaders, or from the news agency, or whether he came down secretly by himself. Whatever the result, we all had the duty to help his investigation. He turned towards Chief Director Wu: "Isn't that right?"

Wu answered in the affirmtive.

"But what's even more important, we have to respect the facts. We have an obligation towards keeping the law. Our close cooperation with the journalist is to help with the investigation and avoid partiality," he said.

11

I hadn't imagined that the Jiang Guangfu case would cause such a sensation. The vice-chairman of the Provincial People's Congress, named Huang, wrote to us wanting information.

I was called into the director's office, where Wu and Lu looked rather perturbed. Wu glanced at the bold ink-brush characters: "I don't know this name. How could I not know him?" he asked.

Lu, however, knew of the man and was able to give his history. He had been an official years ago and then was stripped of his post and didn't have anything to do for years. When the circumstances of his losing his position were examined, they were found to be unjust but he was already over the age limit for his previous position and was promoted instead to this post.

"It proves one thing," Director Wu said. "It is indeed that schoolmaster who is creating havoc."

I was careful not to say too much. I already regretted some of the things I had said before but I guessed that this vice-chairman Huang was behind the journalist and what I had fabricated in my report was actually confirmed. I was relieved to hear that Jiang Guangfu had really written letters of complaint everywhere including this one to the local People's Congress.

Jiang's letter reminded Vice-chairman Huang of a visit he had made nine years before to his school and how he had been impressed with the standards. He had inscribed the school's name-board in his own hand. The headmaster started his letter with the words: "I'm sure you would never have imagined that I am now a prisoner at the bottom end of society." He also described the dispute he had had with Officer Luo on the bus and added a rather trifling afterthought that Luo was the son-in-law of the secretary of the County Committee.

A week before these events had taken place, Officer Luo had married. All four departments of the Judiciary had been invited by Secretary Lu to celebrate his daughter's wedding. The headmaster's name was mentioned and Judge Wu, slightly tipsy, said that the sentence was too light. We thought it was just the wine talking and did not take him too seriously. Lu felt slightly uneasy and said: "The headmaster had not been aware of the real picture, all he did was toss a cigarette to an acquaintance. Furthermore, he had already been punished enough."

Judge Wu disagreed: "This is our county's first case about impeding the handling of public affairs, and we should set a precedent and deal with it harshly. Then the public will better understand the law regarding obstructing an officer of the law in carrying out his duty."

Secretary Lu decided to go to the lavatory at this point, feeling that as he was personally involved, he was at a disadvantage. With him out of the way the case took the form as specified by Judge Wu.

The instructions of Vice-chairman Huang were quite

specific: "If it is found that the complaints are true, you must immediately proclaim his innocence and restore his reputation. Otherwise, how can you face Teacher's Day on September 10?"

Every year people observed Teacher's Day. Sometimes even the handling of criminal cases had to be aware of the date. The previous year, there had been a dispute over a building plot between a teacher and a farmer. The case dragged on for nearly a year with a lot of bickering and ill-will but as soon as September 10 came round, the court was able to pressurise the farmer to give in.

September 10 was not far off. Lu told Judge Wu to keep this in mind, and also reminded him that the People's Standing Committee was the most authoritative organisation in the district. But the judge was stubborn and refused to give way. He said that there was a danger people might concentrate more on the wrongly arrested Xiaofeng rather than the real criminal Xiaolan. "We shouldn't be too rigid. It would be like removing a branch and not the root. Catching the wrong man is a fact, but this was only proved afterwards. The incident on the bus in reality was: a policeman taking a criminal into custody. He was wearing his uniform escorting a man in handcuffs. This was what the passengers saw. As to the actual nature of the case and whether or not he suffered injustice, that is a different matter altogether, but if someone obstructs an officer performing his duty, doesn't that constitute an offence?"

Lu asked if I agreed with what had been said.

I muttered: "In theory, yes."

Lu very prudently suggested that members of the

court discuss the headmaster's case.

At the subsequent meeting, Judge Wu repeated what he had said, but even more expansively, talking for over two hours, and giving no opportunity for anyone to refute his dissertation. It was therefore, unanimously decided to uphold the original sentence handed down to the headmaster.

Lu begged them to reconsider their decision and look at the instructions given out by Vice-chairman Huang.

Wu blocked any further discussion by reminding him that justice cannot be interfered with by anyone or any organisation.

12

The events leading to the headmaster's eventual trial and imprisonment were as follows: he was dragged out of bed in the small hours and handcuffed despite his protests. Only when he was taken to the place where he was to be imprisoned did he quietén down. He recognised it as the training centre for county government officials. He had once given a lecture here as a headmaster and now was a prisoner in the place. He was incarcerated for a month in the detention centre until he came up for trial.

"I want a lawyer," he said. The person handling his case gave him a strange look, but did not reply.

"This is the law," he repeated, "I have the right to a defence."

He was given another look and sarcastically asked if he had taken the wrong medicine.

Secretary Lu headed a team to judge the case. Due to shortage of staff, he transferred all power to members of the public security, the prosecuting department and the courts. But they could not agree as to whether a lawyer should be allowed to defend Jiang Guangfu. Lu was in favour but public opinion of lawyers was not very favourable: "What do lawyers do? They stand against the people and speak for the criminals!" Reluctantly, Lu compromised: "All right, we'll let the lawyer take backstage for the time being."

The headmaster had also mentioned his lack of legal representation in his letter to Vice-chairman Huang.

Judge Wu drafted a letter to Vice-chairman Huang, explaining their decision against a reversal of the case. He asked me to look it over before sending it. "The old man might get angry," he said, "but, we can't let him manipulate the law."

I felt that at least in the writing there were no loopholes. "Very good," I said. "It's almost like a thesis."

The messenger who took the letter said that when the old man read it, he appeared dazed and staggered back. He asked: "Is this judge a graduate of an academy of Government law?"

Wu said: "That seems to prove he has accepted our findings."

The messenger thought that wasn't quite what the old man meant.

"He sat down and dozed off without another word," he said.

13

The journalist had just returned from the capital

when I saw him at the hotel. I asked him: "Do you know of a vice-chairman of the Provincial People's Congress by the name of Huang?"

"There is such a person," he answered.

"You must know him quite well."

"How can that be possible?" he said. "They're the people who are high up, within sight but beyond reach."

I felt he was being too self-abasing and changed the subject. I didn't tell him about the instructions Huang had given. To be truthful I wasn't sure whether the old man was just bored and wanted to poke his nose in other people's business with no real right to do so, and as soon as he met any resistance, all he could do was explode with rage. I didn't want this young journalist to lose heart.

Hao was in a very good mood. He said that all the material needed for the case was in hand. "Tonight I'm going to look over the report and tomorrow I'm going to take it to the County's Standing Committee and listen to their opinions."

"Why bother?" I asked. "Just go your own way. Haven't you done enough?"

"Ah, no," he said, "there's a mystery behind all this!"

He looked excited as he perused the report. I got up to go. "Actually, it's really a fluke I got involved in this case."

He waved a hand in my direction: "Maybe from this meeting my luck will change."

I rang Lu and told him that Hao didn't know Vice-chairman Huang and that his report was finished. I wanted Lu to know as he had taken an active part in the trial of the headmaster. It was he who had announced the fifteen-year sentence.

At the time of the trial, Lu had been exhausted after two nights without sleep. He couldn't keep his eyes open and while Judge Wu was summing up, he was dozing off and didn't wake up until Wu had finished. It was well-known that the case was delicate as it involved Lu's son-in-law, so everyone in the court waited for his response. He rubbed his eyes, unaware of the expectant looks. Judge Wu, who sat beside him said: "Even though this case can't be compared to murder, arson, theft or rape, it is still serious."

Afterwards people decided it was what Judge Wu said that prompted Lu to give such a heavy sentence, despite Wu muttering that it should have been twenty years, not fifteen.

In the following trial of the recidivist, Xiaolan, Lu had no hesitation in pronouncing the death sentence to be carried out immediately.

Xiaolan's execution was a must, as a warning to others like him. He had also boasted about his rape of four young girls, saying: "As I'm going to die anyway, I might as well be shot as a rapist as well as a mugger."

His companion-in-crime had an additional charge of impersonating a police officer and was also sentenced to death.

After these trials were over, our posts changed. I was promoted to judge. Others were promoted from judge to court director and so on.

The one who really had much to celebrate was Judge Wu. In one leap he reached the throne of chief director of the courts of justice.

Chief Director Wu called to me in the hallway. I had expressed my unwillingness to leave my present position, so he said: "We have discussed it further. You can return to the criminal court as before."

He explained that the original decision to move me was to strengthen the other courts, but since I wasn't willing they made other plans.

The scene was just like the last time we stood in the hallway, when he hadn't finished what he was going to say. But this time he completed the sentence.

"The court's mid-level staff have all been reorganised," he said. "From now on you'll be responsible for all the work that goes on in the criminal court."

I was astonished. I had not dreamt I would become court director as well.

As he told me, Wu was wiping the sweat off his forehead. He had just come from a County Committee meeting where he related the outcome of Hao's investigations.

Secretary Lu wanted to accept it, but the majority of the council members were against. They felt the journalist had not been objective enough and what he had written was unclear. They also did not like the tone of it.

Wu had repeated what he had said before but slightly more restrained and succinct. This time he only spoke for about an hour and then stopped.

Hao hadn't agreed saying he was not prepared to listen to an academic report. He said that what was in front of them was not something abstract; not a painting, not a group of sculptures, but a case involving live people.

He mentioned three "ifs": if the headmaster had not tossed the cigarette to Xiaofeng when it landed on Officer Luo's lap, if, when Luo was about to light up, the headmaster had let it go and thought of it as doing a stranger a favour; if Xiaofeng was being escorted by an ordinary policeman and not Officer Luo who had a special status... and so on.

Secretary Lu had coughed and interrupted him: "I absolutely agree with this journalist's opinions, this isn't an academic discussion." He criticised Chief Director Wu, saying: "Too many theories tangled together make it easy to fall into sophistry without being able to solve the real problem."

The journalist summarised the whole events leading to the headmaster's arrest even citing the false arrest of Xiaofeng.

Xiaofeng had not imagined that he was under arrest and that as a result it would involve the headmaster. He couldn't think of what wrong he had done and only after interrogation did he confess that he had once stolen a water melon.

"Time, place, amount!" the interrogator roared.

"When I was eight years old. There wasn't a village then, only a watermelon field. I stole the watermelon and ate it when the adults were not looking."

It was only then that the mistaken identity was realised and Secretary Lu gave the chief of the Public Security Bureau a reprimand.

It was going home time when I remembered the message: "Chief Director Wu," I said, "someone wanted me to send your their greetings."

"Who?"

"Didn't we handle an bigamy case in Jiangdian Village eight years ago?"

He remembered: "It was a woman called Hu Youxiang," he said.

"She wants you to take some time off and have dinner with her," I said. "Gou'er also send his greetings. You wouldn't recognise them now." I described their prosperous life.

He sighed and shook his head: "Who would have thought it?"

Someone called out that there was a phone call for me. It was Hao telling me about the council's decision despite General Secretary Lu's advice.

He told me what the committee had said, which was summed up in two phrases and ten words: inconsistent with the facts, disapprove publishing it in the papers.

"It's not what you wanted," I said.

"Just the opposite," he replied. "It's just what I wanted. Didn't I promise to tell you my mystery before I left? Come to the hotel now."

"When are you leaving?" I asked.

"Tomorrow afternoon, I already have my ticket."

"Then I'll see you tomorrow," I said, "at the station when I see you off."

Matters took a drastic turn the morning he was due to leave. A ruling from the provincial High Court arrived and Chief Director Wu's face turned deathly pale when he read it. He dragged me to Lu's home where he was just finishing breakfast. "This case is a lot more complicated than I imagined it to be," he commented.

Wu said: "In all probability, Jiang Guangfu has already been freed."

Lu became more alert: "Are you suggesting that the lower courts have to follow the decision of the High Courts?"

It was true. The People's High Court's white paper had black characters and a bright red seal stamped on it, rescinding our original decision and pronounced the headmaster innocent of all charges.

Lu suggested that Wu should get in touch with someone in the Provincial High Court. An acquaintance was quickly found, an assistant judge, who commented: "Of all people to offend, why the Provincial People's Congress Vice-chairman Huang, that stubborn old man?"

He said that Huang had been a recognised authority on law. To discuss law with him was like showing one's slight skill in front of an expert. Though he had retired from active law practice, he was indeed an old tree with its roots deeply embedded. He had trained a solid group of contingents to take up where he had left off.

"That old man is very stubborn. He's determined to uphold justice, he even dares to poke a hole in the sky."

The assistant judge guessed that the headmaster had probably been released and returned home and suggested we try to appease him.

Lu immediately called for another meeting of the council. He praised Hao's report saying: "When one goes against the law, one must pay the price. When one is wrong, one must change. Why do we lack the courage to admit when we are wrong?"

This was the first time his colleagues had seen him

so fired up and they listened in silence.

He continued: "The investigative report is completely in line with the facts. I agree to its being published. We have a responsibility toward the provincial court to examine our part in this case and take measures to improve our work."

He added solemnly: "The County Committee will use the Jiang Guangfu case as a lesson."

Officer Luo accompanied me to the station when I went to see Hao off.

He introduced himself to the journalist who already guessed who he was by his big physique. Officer Luo said his father-in-law had asked him to go to the station. "Come back often. You will be very welcome." he said warmly, which seemed in stark contrast to his normal behaviour. Then rather embarrassedly he said: "I am very sorry I played such an ignominious role in the headmaster's case."

Hao didn't hear him. He was busy looking at the decision of the High Court in astonishment. "How did this come about?" he asked.

"My father-in-law wanted you to know that he had insisted on holding another council meeting and again expressed appreciation of your report. This time his opinion was accepted and the county also acknowledges your version of the case and will learn from it."

I sat in the bus next to Hao waiting until it started to move. He kept repeating what a good man I was and he would never forget me. "We must keep in touch," he said.

I only listened with half an ear. Officer Luo was standing by the door waiting to wave him off. There was another twenty minutes to go. I mused: A journalist has been here and is about to go. Time passes just like that, but within this short time, things have happened. That which seemed straightforward, got complicated and confusing. Like in this case, a journalist came because someone suffered an injustice. He was finally exonerated, not because of the journalist. And me, for example, I got through the hard times, went back and forth from the criminal court and then returned and even got promoted. Hao nudged me and asked: "What are you thinking about? Don't worry, the report will be published soon."

He was waiting for me to ask him about the mystery he had promised to tell me. After a while he spoke of it without my prompting. He said he knew that after the publication of the investigation, there would be a sensation but just one explosion is not enough. One must go out on a second, a third, the more the better, and all the county decision did was to serve that purpose. His wish had been fulfilled.

"What's worth celebrating is the dramatic change in the tone of the county decision," he said. "The first report objectively described the unjustness of the case and let readers see how absurd it all was. The second report was a result of a journalist's interest and their rejection of his findings. It let the readers see how even more absurd it was and the third report was written about the County decision to right the wrongs overnight, it let the readers …"

He was so excited and his voice became so loud passengers stared at him. One gave him a look of disgust. I sighed, everyone has their moments when they become dizzy with success. I wondered whether he would write to me after he returned or was this our last farewell?

At last the bus began to move. I shook his hand through the window. His eyelids were red. "Do you know what great problem of mine it would solve if the report were a success?" he asked.

I saw him stop and suddenly stare at something behind me. I looked round and saw the passenger who had given him such look of disgust return his stare and then spit on the ground in disdain.

Hao's body stretched out from the window. He yelled: "I'll write and tell you about it!"

16

Officer Luo and I caught up with the bus as it travelled towards the provincial capital. I showed Hao the warrant. When he read it his face went pale. I said: "Sign here." His hand shook as he signed. We had chased after the bus for about three hours in the police car, sirens blaring and managed to stop the bus by the bridge. I had walked to his seat and told him to get down. Hao could see by my face that things looked bad for him. He steadied his hand on the rail as his legs became weak.

It was a coincidence that as the bus left, a passenger recognised him. It was the one who had spat on the ground. He was on his way home from the provincial capital and Officer Luo heard him mutter: "Hell, this fellow has come down here to fool around." Luo asked him why he was so scornful of such an important journalist from the city. The passenger spat again:

"Him a journalist?" and then went on to explain that Hao worked in the same food factory as he did. He had not been satisfied with his job and hung around the editor of the news agency. He had had a few measly articles published and then thought he was good enough to switch jobs. He forced the agency to hire him on a temporary basis and tried to curry favour with the top people so that he could get a permanent post.

"You mean to say, he's an employee of your factory," officer Luo asked, "and not with the news agency?"

"Transferring to the news agency is just a dream of his. No one likes him in the factory and he doesn't have the qualifications for a transfer."

Luo dragged me to Secretary Lu's office who frowned at us both. There was another man in the room. His face was so pale it gave off a yellowish tinge and was puffy. When he turned his head round, I almost cried out his name: "Jiang Guangfu."

Lu continued speaking to the headmaster. "You will be reimbursed for all your economic losses," he said. "The County will hold separate meetings at Jianggang Village and the county's educational committee to publicly announce the misjudgment of your case and to restore your reputation. He continued in a mollifying tone: "You have stayed at this village too long. You ought to make a move. You could come to the county government and take up a more important post. For instance in the education committee as a vice-director, or become head of a middle school.

We told Lu what the passenger had said and he immediately telephoned the news agency who verified what had been said about Hao. A new head of the agency had been appointed and had dismissed all part-time workers.

The odds were certainly against Hao as he sat in the police car, his head bowed, not saying a word. He reminded me of the second criminal who had been sentenced to death and I wondered if he hated me now. I realised that if I had not been on duty, "Journalist" Hao would not have had an easy time with Officer Luo, who had a short fuse.

Luo stopped the car outside the court building. He wanted to escort Hao from the main street to the detention centre so that everybody could take a good look at this false journalist.

Chief Director Wu was coming out from the building and walking by his side was the headmaster, looking much better. Hao stumbled in front of the two men as he was dragged out of the car.

The headmaster said to Wu: "People are all talking about the person who posed as a journalist and came here to practise his chicanery, fooling the court and Provincial government. Is this the man?"

"That's him," the Chief Director replied.

The scene of the two main characters made me lose myself in thought. Vice-chairman Huang had eventually saved the headmaster. Why not write a letter to him and tell him about "journalist" Hao's fate? I reasoned: If there were something amiss maybe he would, as before, take up the cudgels and rectify the wrong.

Translated by Eileen Cheng
Revised by Esther Samson

The Drowning of Jiuzhou City

ONCE upon a time there was a big city named Jiuzhou, with nine districts. Alas, it was swallowed up in a great flood long ago.

The records show that centuries later, the great lake beneath whose waters the city lies buried, dried up in a fierce drought of a magnitude which occurs only once in several centuries. Local people started digging for water in the middle of the bed of the dried-up lake, and while they dug they came upon the old city wall of Jiuzhou. The wall was built of dark green blocks as big as paving stones. Sadly, that very night came a sudden torrential rainstorm, which solved the water shortage but also completely refilled the lake, leaving the drowned city again buried at the bottom.

The original flood disaster which befell the city had a lot to do with a rich medicine dealer's worship of Buddha.

His medicine shop was the largest business in the city. He sold only one medicine. Though its price was low, it was a cure-all. As the richest person in Jiuzhou he was reputed to have a huge fortune. He could have bought an entire city just by snapping his fingers, had he wished. After he arrived in Jiuzhou, the wealth of the locality had incessantly flowed into his house.

The dealer was very frugal. He ate nothing but common vegetables. He wore a cotton-padded robe in winter, a short garment in summer and a black gown in spring and autumn. He spent all his money on the worship of Buddha. He gave money to cover the cost of joss sticks, lamp oil and daily necessities of monks, and for the rebuilding of temples and statues of Buddha. He was very pious. Besides generous donations, every day he went to a different temple by rota to offer sacrifices.

The man was not a native of Jiuzhou. He had come from far away. One day in his home city, he picked up a scrap of paper. After several readings he decided it was a prescription for a medicine. He thought it was an elixir that could save people all over the world. But no-one believed him. Instead he was charged with cheating people by selling fake medicine and was put into prison. Some of his friends broke into the prison and freed him. He thanked them and left for Jiuzhou with his two best friends — and the prescription.

They underwent many hardships on their journey. When they reached the Gobi Desert, with its boundless rolling sand, the man thought they had come to the end of the world. He feared that none of them would survive if they walked on, fearful that their stocks of food and water would not be enough for the three of them. So he abandoned one of his friends and continued his way to Jiuzhou with the other. The road led to a huge swamp. The boundless barren tract again made the man think he was on a thin line between life and death. He again feared that they would not survive, and abandoned the other friend. After all the tribulations he finally reached firm ground and saw Jiuzhou City ahead full of fine houses. He found that he still had more than enough food and water, and bitterly regretted that he had abandoned his two friends. But it was too late. The man settled down in Jiuzhou and employed new hands to help him. He produced the pills according to the prescription. The cure-all pills soon found a ready market and quickly made him the richest man in Jiuzhou.

But he was deeply troubled. He felt that he owed a great debt for what he now regarded as his selfish decisions in leaving his friends to their fate. Yet here he was, prospering and getting richer by the day, far and away the richest person in the city. At first he could think of no explanation for what he thought was his undeserved good fortune. Finally he decided that he must be specially favoured by some god or spirit. This thought still left him perturbed, until he resolved to worship Buddha. He could not decide which particular god was protecting him. So he worshipped every holy statue in Jiuzhou, whether of clay or wood.

One night, a silver-haired old man with a white beard appeared in his dream. The dealer thought he was one of the gods or spirits he had been worshipping, because he looked very familiar. With a very godly air, the old man told him that his sincerity had moved the heavens.

"I'll tell you a top secret," the old man said, smoothing his beard. "The City of Jiuzhou will be submerged at the bottom of a lake."

The medicine dealer prostrated himself on the ground, kowtowing.

"There's a barren hill outside the East Gate, on

which lies a pile of stones. Among the stones is a stone lion. The city shall sink on the day the lion's eyes turn red.''

The dealer first thought of all the inhabitants. With a low kowtow he asked: ''Is there a way to escape?''

''When the deluge comes, the lucky ones shall hear the words 'Drowning! Drowning!' You will survive if you swim in the direction of the voice.''

The old man stopped talking, and as the dealer looked up from the ground, the old man gradually faded away. The dealer woke up.

The rich dealer was careful and conscientious by nature. He made the cure-all pills in a highly secretive way. He had workshops in different places, each bearing a different name, each run independently and producing just one of the components, and the final, most important components were made by himself. He sold his medicine for very little profit though it was highly effective in curing illnesses. Feeling threatened, the city's other medicine dealers united to fight against him, but in vain. They finally had to give up and change their trades.

After three days and nights' continuous thinking, the medicine dealer worked out a watertight strategy against the threatened flood. He secretly put everything in order. He got up early every morning and went to look at the eyes of the stone lion before burning incense at the temples by turns. He became one of the earliest birds in Jiuzhou.

On the barren hill the medicine dealer was observed one day by a pig-slaughterer.

Every day the slaughterer got up when the dew lay on the ground, the morning mist still hung in the air

and the sky in the east had a streak of white light.
One morning as he was returning without a care in the
world through the East Gate, he saw a black shadow
pass by.

He followed, thinking it might be a thief who had
been in hiding for a long time as Jiuzhou had been
without crime for several years and the city gates were
usually left wide open. The slaughterer thought the
thief might be looking for his loot which he had buried
in the hill and now, feeling safe but poor, decided to re-
trieve it.

The slaughterer thought to frighten the thief into
giving him a share of this imagined treasure, so he
clasped his double-bladed knife tightly in one hand
while holding a piece of bloody pig's offal a grateful
customer had given him in his other. He did stop and
think for a second that the thief might be savage and
try to kill him, but then he smiled as he remembered
he had dealt with squealing and struggling pigs and
was quite strong himself.

The slaughterer hid among the stones and watched.
As the dawn became lighter he discerned a human figure going up the steps towards the stone lion. That is
a good place to hide the treasure, thought the
slaughterer, and his heart began to pound with
excitement.

The figure paused in front of the stone lion but the
slaughterer, who could see everything quite clearly from
his hiding place, was very disappointed to see him just
stare at the lion's eyes and return the way he had
come.

He met the medicine dealer at the beancurd inn on
East Street. The dealer called for a bowl of jellied

beancurd. The proprietor was quite surprised because usually it was the slaughterer who came first, but this time he was the second customer. They sat together at the same table silently eating their jellied beancurd.

This particular jellied beancurd inn was unique in Jiuzhou, almost comparable to the medicine shop in reputation. Some time before, the other beancurd sellers had tasted it, panicked and then went back to their own premises and knocked them down and did something else for a living. Thus the beancurd inn on East Street provided all the restaurants as well as customers with their delicious jellied beancurd. Customers would begin to fill the inn as soon as the sun came out and there would be queues of people waiting until the day grew dark and the inn closed.

It was owned by an elderly couple with neither children nor employees. The kitchen was very small and people were puzzled how the couple managed to make such tasty beancurd yet never saw them buy the raw ingredients.

Soon the slaughterer and the medicine dealer became friends. The slaughterer suspected that his new friend's wealth could not have come just from the cheap pills he sold but that he must be a thief, and the selling of pills was just a cover.

The slaughterer was very skilled with pigs. He would scratch the pig's ears before adroitly turning it over on its back, then place his foot down to steady the pig and stab it through the throat.

He was a canny man and knew the ways of the world. So every morning he would follow the medicine dealer as he climbed up to the stone lion, see him stare at the lion's eyes and then turn away. Finally the slaughterer's patience came to an end. He decided to jump out and deal with the medicine dealer the same way he dealt with pigs and scratch his neck with the knife. Then he would know the truth.

The next morning, the slaughterer did as he had planned but the medicine dealer just looked at him fearlessly and said in a friendly tone: "Oh it's you! How come you're here?" The slaughterer's desire to kill went away.

Together they went down the hill to the beancurd inn.

One day the medicine dealer revealed the secret. "The City of Jiuzhou will suffer an unprecedented disaster," he said. "The day the lion's eyes turn red is the day the city will sink."

By this time the slaughterer had decided the medicine dealer was a little mad. He had heard about his giving all his money to the ghosts and spirits and now he was coming out with all this rubbish. He was glad he had not killed him for nothing, so he pretended he believed the story and asked: "Is there a way out?"

"When the city sinks into the water, a voice will shout 'Drowning! Drowning!' You will stay alive if you swim in that direction," the dealer answered.

The slaughterer never followed the man again but continued walking in the morning dew and mist, greeting the medicine dealer loudly at the first ray of daylight before going on to the old couple's inn and eating the first bowl of jellied beancurd, laughing as he imagined the picture of the dealer in front of the stone lion on top of the barren hill.

Meanwhile the medicine dealer was sure the day was drawing near. He started to carry out his original plan.

He allocated one third of his employees for other pur-
poses. They were all loud-voiced, strong and quick.
He divided the city into nine districts and told them to
familiarise themselves with every street and alley. His second step was to put half of them to the same task but
suddenly became very agitated and rejected the whole
plan. He told all his employees to stop manufacturing
the pills and provided them with a special suit, a copper gong and a horse and told them to learn to ride before putting them back into the nine districts.

The people of Jiuzhou city were curious and a little
disturbed to see groups of people of all shapes and
sizes walking about in the same clothes bearing the
name of the medicine shop. As it was the only shop of
its kind in the area they thought it rather strange and
unnecessary.

The slaughterer and dealer continued to bump into
each other below the barren hill as they went their separate ways.

The weather began to change and it got hotter and
hotter and there was a drought. Thousands of square
kilometres of land dried up like rocks. The fields had
nothing but dry grass in them. Fissures appeared in
the ground so wide that children could stand between
them. The slaughterer continued getting up as early as
before to slaughter the pigs but his heart was heavy.
They still met at the bottom of the hill and though he
wanted to, he could not laugh at the medicine dealer.

One day the slaughterer had only one pig to slaughter and so he had plenty of time on his hands. He
looked to the east: the sky was as black as the bottom
of a smoked pot. He stood below the barren hill
hesitating. Then he had an idea. He walked up the

steps towards the stone lion and stained its eyes with fresh pig's blood. Smiling to himself he went away. Meanwhile the medicine dealer was sure doomsday was imminent and was more frightened and worried than ever before. He stumbled up the steps and rushed to the stone lion. He stared closely at the lion's eyes and saw they were truly red. He felt them with his hands and smelt blood. He believed that the stone lion was not only red-eyed but also shedding tears of blood.

He hurried back to his workshop and gathered all his employees together and told them to put on their special clothes, ride their horses banging the gongs and shout: "The city's being drowned!"

Horses could be heard galloping through the cobble-stone streets, raising bright sparks from the clattering hooves. But the people just stood around listening to their shouts:

"The city's being drowned!"

"The city's being drowned!"

"The　— city's　— being　— drowned!"

By evening the city was still motionless and people were standing around watching. The medicine dealer bade his men to stop and he brought out his white horse and with the largest copper gong in his hand, and accompanied by two burly employees holding torches, charged through the streets shouting the same warning: "The city's sinking in water!"

By two o'clock in the morning his voice had gone and the torches burnt down during the darkest hour of the night. Heaven and earth seemed merged into darkness. The medicine dealer was in despair. Suddenly a brilliant light appeared and the city of Jiuzhou grew as bright as day. Everyone began to panic and prepared to escape.

Only the slaughterer remained calm. He did not think that two dabs of pig's blood could topple the world. He looked up and down. Even if there were to be three days of continuous downpour the drought would not end and the fissures in the earth would still remain. He continued to carry on as usual and went to the beancurd inn, calling for his bowl of jellied beancurd. But the inn was strangely quiet and empty. He looked into the kitchen and saw the old couple were trying to move a water vat. They were the last to flee the city, caring only for their water vat which contained the raw materials. This was the first time the slaughterer saw the water vat. It was shaped like a waist drum, and was painted red and yellow and carved with ten weaving whirling dragons. In the vat lay all the secrets of the beancurd inn. It was always half full with soybeans soaking in water and nobody knew why it never increased or decreased.

The slaughterer realised how valuable the vat was.

He wiped his hands, clasped the edge of the vat and moved it. A great round hole so deep it was impossible to see the bottom, was revealed.

White mist suddenly shot up into the air, growing thicker and bluer. The blue air turned into whirlpools becoming more and more rapid. Suddenly a freezing cold made their flesh and bones feel as if their souls were being snatched away. "Run!" he shouted.

The blue air leapt up again, spurting and splashing and shooting great white waves into the sky. The roof was torn away and the momentum of the water swept up into the sky engulfing the sun, turning from scarlet to brown and then black. Heaven and earth merged into one and a floating light loomed on the horizon. A boundless sea surged forward as the light grew brighter.

The slaughterer was the only survivor. After struggling for several days and nights in the water, he heard the words: "Drowning! Drowning!" He swam towards the sound and managed to find a bank overgrown with verdant grass.

He survived and brought up a family and called the place where he landed Anle, which means Peace and Happiness. In Anle there is a lake. Under the lake is the drowned city of Jiuzhou.

Translated by Wang Chiying
Revised by Esther Samson

图书在版编目(CIP)数据

秋菊打官司：英文/ 陈源斌著；Walling A. 等译 .－北京：
中国文学出版社，1994.10
ISBN 7－5071－0277－7

I.秋... II.①陈... ② W... III.①中篇小说－作品集
－中国－当代－英文 ② 短篇小说－作品集－中国－当
代－英文 IV.I247.7

中国版本图书馆 CIP 数据核字(94)第 11432 号

秋菊打官司

陈源斌

熊猫丛书

*

中国文学出版社出版
（中国北京百万庄路 24 号）
中国国际图书贸易总公司发行
（中国北京车公庄西路 35 号）
北京邮政信箱第 399 号　　邮政编码 100044
1995 年 第 1 版（英）
1997年第 2 次印刷
ISBN 7－5071－0277－7
02400
10－E－2929 P